REVENANT

A Montague and Strong Detective Novel

ORLANDO A. SANCHEZ

ABOUT THE STORY

There's no way back...past the point of no return.

Monty and Simon survived the Stormblood, but not without grave consequences. Whatever method York used to complete the ritual opened a door to something ancient, dark, and evil.

A Revenant.

Now, that Revenant is hunting them. It needs their life force to be completely free.

There's only one way to get it.

Eliminate them both.

Together, they must face this new threat before it becomes too powerful to stop and destroys them all.

"For life and death are one, even as the river and the sea are one."
-Kahlil Gibran

"Whoever fights monsters should see to it that in the process he does not become a monster."
-Nietzsche

ONE

"Are you certain you don't wish to join us?" Monty asked as Dex created a large, green circle in the center of our reception area. "Your insight may be crucial."

"Aye, a fair point," Dex said, focused on the circle on the floor. "If I want to be alive to provide future insight, I best make sure to pay Mo a visit before I join you."

"You're not actually scared of her, are you?" I asked. "I mean, yes, she's up there in 'scare your heart still' territory, but you aren't really scared of her."

Dex gave me a wide smile.

"Are you scared of vampires?" he asked, still smiling. "Do you lay awake at night wondering if they will attack?"

"Not really, no," I said. "I mean, I think I can handle myself enough to deal with a vampire."

"I feel the same way," he said as he gestured, causing more symbols to appear in the circle. "Vampires hold no fear for me. Now, Goddesses"—he gave me a wink—"especially those known as Death Goddesses, well, those deserve a healthy respect. Don't you think?"

I nodded.

"So you're scared of her," I said with a smile. "It's okay to admit it, you know."

He laughed.

"Shame is not one of the qualities I'm familiar with, but I'll ask you a question in return, before you go. Fair enough?"

He motioned for me, Monty, and Peaches to enter the circle

"Sure," I said, stepping into the green circle as Peaches bumped my hip with his enormous head and nearly sent me tumbling across the floor. At this point, I was beginning to think his "accidental" nudges were no accident. "Ask away."

"You're not scared of vampires, you say, correct?"

I nodded.

"On the whole, no, not really. Why?"

Dex began gesturing as the symbols in the circle rotated and began to glow brighter.

"How about an ancient vampire, powerful enough to face an entire horde of vampires on her own?" he asked, his face serious now. "A vampire powerful enough to not only keep several clans of vampires in check, but numerous packs of wolves, and an enclave of mages as well—all together forming a council that could rival any sect on the plane and some off-plane. A vampire that barely fears the dawn because of her power. Would you fear *that* vampire?"

A chill ran down my spine. I knew who he was referring to.

Michiko.

"Well, I, well..."

"I see," Dex said, nodding sagely as the wicked smile returned. "You understand perfectly. Give my regards to TK and LD. I will be there *after* I see Mo."

I nodded mutely as the circle erupted with green light, blinding me. When I could see again, we were standing in a large, cramped shop.

Fordey Boutique.

The marble floor was covered with boxes and crates of every size. On the walls, warped shelves that appeared on the verge of collapse strained under the weight of the items taking up every available inch of space.

"You walked right into that one," Monty said, brushing off his sleeves. "It's best to stay away from the Morrigan as a topic of discussion with my uncle."

"He doesn't like talking about her?"

"On the contrary," Monty said, peering into the distance. "He absolutely relishes regaling anyone who will listen to his escapades."

"She doesn't mind?"

"On occasion, *she* is the one telling the story, much to his delight."

"Those two are made for each other."

"Indeed," he said. "He does enjoy sharing every sordid detail."

"That's been my experience," I said, looking around the quiet shop. "Then what is the problem? I mean, aside from his allergy to clothing and the visuals he tries to give me?"

I shuddered at some of the memories.

"There is a line that shouldn't be crossed," Monty said, narrowing his eyes as he looked to the right. "The family once tried to prohibit my uncle from being with the Morrigan."

I chuckled until I realized he was being serious.

"You're serious?" I asked, surprised. "They tried to tell Dex what to do with his love life?"

Monty nodded, still focused on a point somewhere in the distance.

"Long ago, when my father was still alive, my uncle was more, shall we say, malleable," Monty said, heading down the familiar narrow corridor. "He listened to my father, valued his advice. Even took instruction from him every now and then."

"What happened?"

"You can't control who you love," Monty said. "After a particularly bloody battle, he met *her*."

"He met the Morrigan on the battlefield?" I asked, mildly shocked. "She left him alive?"

"Love at first sight, or so I'm told, if you believe in such things," Monty replied, pulling up a small stool. "Everyone in the family lost their collective minds, except my father."

"Why was your father okay with it?"

"Several reasons," Monty said. "My father was a wise man. He knew my uncle better than anyone. He also knew that trying to prevent him from being with the Morrigan was futile, so he did the most logical thing."

"Which was?"

"He got out of the way and gave him one piece of advice."

"Sounds like your dad was similar to Dex in many ways," I said, wishing I had met Connor Montague when he had been alive. "What did he tell Dex?"

"If she makes you happy, bollocks to anyone who says different. You can't control who you love."

"Wow," I said, mildly surprised. "Kind of raw, but still, honest."

"They were brothers, after all. My father had his crude side, which is why they got along so well," Monty said with the hint of a smile. "Dex took his advice and told the family elders to stuff it."

"That must have gone over well," I said. "What did they do?"

"The Montagues are a powerful mage family going back for millennia," Monty said. "They tried...*force*."

I winced.

"Sounds like a bad idea."

"It was," he said. "This was some time ago, but my uncle has always been one of the strongest in the family. They thought they could confront him collectively. They were mistaken."

"Your uncle faced them alone and beat them?"

"Not alone," Monty said. "The Morrigan joined his side. She loved—and still loves—him, and he loves her. I don't pretend to understand it, but I don't question it...ever. I merely accept it, and her, as part of my family. If she makes him happy, that's all that matters."

"Shit," I muttered. "Facing Dex alone is bad enough. I can't imagine facing the both of them."

"It was a brief, violent *conversation*," Monty said. "In the end, the family agreed it was in everyone's best interest to leave my uncle to his own devices."

"I bet," I said, looking around for the proprietors of the shop. "Where are they? Did they know we were coming?"

"We wouldn't be inside Fordey if they didn't," Monty said. "My uncle would never violate their active defenses. If we're in here, they know."

"I knew I felt a disturbance," I heard LD say in the distance. "Our guests are here."

I saw TK appear at the end of the corridor. She didn't look pleased, which meant I should be concerned.

"Monty, she looks pissed. Did you do something again?"

"I think we both did this time," he said, keeping his voice low. "Let me handle this."

She gave us both a long look and turned on her heel, leaving us where we were. LD waved us to follow him. TK walked ahead while LD hung back.

"She looks pissed," I said. "Why does she look pissed?"

"That's not pissed," LD said, glancing up at TK. "Pissed was a few days ago when she felt whatever it is York did to you two. That was pissed. I had to close off part of the Boutique. Well, what's left of it."

"What made her that upset?"

"Where do I start?" LD said with a sigh, rubbing a hand through his hair. "Lost elder blood rune activated, Chaos being in play, you two going off to see Tempest without extending her an invitation at the very least, Verity is now on your asses...Oh, and that small matter of York kicking off a Stormblood, somehow pulling it off in some insane maneuver only York could do. Did I miss anything?"

"If you did," I said, "I don't think it would be smart to add to that list."

"Ahh," LD said with a nod. "You're finally learning. Don't worry. Even if I missed something, she won't."

Somehow, those words did not fill me with anything approaching comfort.

"She knows?" I asked, as LD gave me a look that plainly said: *How are you still alive?* "How?"

"Yes, she knows. Everyone in the Ten knows. We make it a point to stay informed with one another. Helps keep the world safe and all of us alive. Especially something like this."

"Wait a minute," I said, holding up a hand as we kept walking down several corridors. "Why would she be upset at us? We didn't *do* anything."

LD glanced at Monty as we kept moving.

"You want to tell him, or should I?" LD asked as he rubbed Peaches' head. "He should know."

"She's more upset at me than at you," Monty said. "Because the lost rune I used was quite dangerous."

"I thought all lost runes were dangerous?"

"This one was particularly volatile," Monty said after a pause, and then looked at LD. "York managed the Stormblood without negative consequence."

"Tristan, you're young, but you're not *that* young," LD said, shaking his head. "The lost elder *blood* rune was the rune of seals. You have no idea what you set off. Well, not you exactly—York—but also you. Verity is the least of your problems, *our* problems."

"What are you talking about?" Monty asked. "The Stormblood was successful. York managed it without activating the rune in its entirety."

"That would be incorrect," TK said as we arrived in a large, circular room that was mostly white marble covered in runes. It vaguely reminded me of the room where York had trapped us to perform the Stormblood ritual. "He was rushed, which meant he was sloppy."

"What is this place?" I asked, looking around. "I've never been in this room."

TK looked down at Peaches, formed a large sausage and rubbed his head as he stepped to one side with his prize between his jaws. It wasn't just her expression that set me on edge. She was dressed in black combat armor with the usual black-on-black accents, and her hair was pulled back in a loose ponytail.

It was her eyes that made me pause.

They were extra green.

Her eyes were normally green, but this time they gave off a subtle glow. It wasn't the *look at how amazing my eyes are* kind of glow. It was closer to the *my eyes will be the last thing you see before I evaporate you* kind of glow.

LD was dressed in mage casual: an off-white dress shirt with black slacks and comfortable house shoes. I took a step closer to LD, just in case the orbs were going to start flying.

"This room is a dampener," TK said, turning to face Monty. "Similar to the one York probably used to perform the Stormblood ritual. We will need it to conduct an audit and see how much damage was done."

She waved a hand, and the runes in the walls came to life with orange energy.

"Damage?" Monty said. "What damage?"

"No," TK said, that one word a blade that sliced through any following response. "I will be asking the questions now."

"Understood," Monty said with a curt nod. "Please continue."

"You found a lost elder blood rune. Where?"

Monty flexed his jaw, but remained calm. The tension in the room was a physical presence, charging the air with energy. Monty was perhaps stronger now since the last time he had faced TK in a reckoning, but I doubted he was strong enough to take her, even with Peaches' and my help.

Besides, we weren't feeling particularly suicidal today.

"The Living Library," Monty said. "Portal access to a self-contained section of the Library."

She glanced at LD, who nodded.

"That was the recent breach Ziller reported," LD said. "Nothing was removed."

"Except the elder rune," TK said. "Please secure the Library, dear."

"Of course. Be right back," LD said and disappeared with a gesture.

"Please stand next to each other," TK said, turning to us. "I need to examine what York did."

I stood next to Monty.

"York is insane," she said with a frown. "I can't believe he did this."

"York is dead," I said. "Part of the museum fell on him."

"I'll believe that when I see his body."

LD reappeared a few moments later.

"Living Library secured," he said. "Ziller extends his thanks and requests this." He handed her a piece of paper. "No rush."

"I should hope not," she said, glancing at the paper before incinerating it with a thought. "We won't have one for at least another decade."

"I told him as much," LD answered as he circled us. "He said as soon as we get it would be fine."

She nodded and continued examining us with narrowed eyes.

"How bad is it?" LD asked, narrowing his eyes at us. "I can see the bonds, but there's much I don't see. Definitely a Stormblood, that's for sure."

"This was the trigger," TK said with a frown as she cocked her head to one side. "The bonds are solid, but the lattices he used drew on the power of the elder rune. It's ingenious in its madness. No other mage could have done this. The connections are elegant, yet completely unorthodox. We can't unravel this."

"No other mage we know would have attempted something like this," LD said, holding up a finger. "Oh, wait. Maybe one."

TK nodded.

"Dex has done things in a similar vein with his teleportation, but nothing on this scale," she said. "York has outdone himself and doomed us all."

"You ever seen a shared Stormblood?"

"No, I've never seen a twinned Stormblood," TK said, peering at us as she moved her fingers through the air. "This part here, see it?"

LD stepped to the location TK indicated and nodded.

"Looks like a nexus," he said. "You think that did it?"

"I think so. It's very irregular. One moment." She held up a finger and moved it in the space between me and Monty. "Let me see what Tempest thinks of this."

She created a green teleportation circle and vanished a moment later. I looked at LD.

"Did she actually just go to visit Josephine?" I asked. "Without an invite or announcing she was coming?"

LD nodded.

"Probably the only person on this, or any other plane, who can do that," LD said, shaking his head as he looked at Monty. "What possessed you to use an elder rune? A lost elder blood rune?"

"Extenuating circumstances," Monty said. "We were facing an agent of Chaos. Our options were limited."

LD stared at Monty.

"Don't try to hustle a hustler, hombre," LD said. "You wanted to know if it would work. At the very least admit it. You *wanted* to unleash the power."

"Yes," Monty admitted. "That was part of it. The greater part was avoiding our imminent death."

"*Your* imminent death, you mean," LD said, glancing at me. "I doubt Strong was going to have an issue with dying, being death challenged and all."

"Be that as it may, even Simon was in danger, despite his current affliction," Monty replied. "Mahnes was a real threat to us all."

"So you felt the need to use this rune," LD continued. "Which helped you defeat Mahnes, the agent of Chaos, yes?"

"Yes, but unfortunately we were unable to banish or entrap Chaos."

TK appeared a moment later.

"Show me the rune you used, exactly," she said. "Omit nothing."

Monty traced the rune in the air. LD's eyes opened wider as he hissed.

"Hombre, that rune...that rune is bad news," he said, his face becoming slightly pale. "I'm surprised you're still alive."

TK sighed and gestured. The runes in the room dimmed around us. She suddenly looked exhausted. She exchanged a few glances with LD and I could sense that I was missing something, something that was potentially apocalyptic.

"You truly are your uncle's nephew," she said after a

moment. "A talisman was required for the blood ritual. What was it?"

"Yes," Monty said. "I formed a ring. We used it on Mahnes."

"This ring," she said. "Whose blood was used?"

"I thought Stark created the ring?" I said.

"Stark created the framework," Monty said. "The rune and the blood completed his work and imbued it with power."

"The blood?" I asked, concerned. "Whose blood, Monty?"

"My blood," he said. "My blood gave it the final shape."

"But Jarman? Mahnes-Chaos drained her dry."

"No. The ring was ready before Jarman sacrificed herself," Monty said, turning to TK. "How bad is it?"

TK looked away, but I could feel the controlled energy and anger radiating out from where she stood. If her current energy was any indicator, we had raced past bad and entered horrific. From the looks they gave each other, horrific was a pit stop on the way to Armageddon.

"An elder rune of sealing is like a door," LD said. "Sometimes this door allows something in, rather than keeping things out."

"Allows something in?" I asked. "What exactly are you talking about?"

"We're not exactly certain," TK said. "Somehow between using the elder rune and York performing the Stormblood ritual, a door was opened. A door that never should have been opened."

Ice slowly filled my veins.

"What walked in?"

TK gave LD another glance, an entire unspoken discussion in the space of a blink.

"A Revenant," she said finally. "One that's coming for both of you, it seems."

TWO

"Impossible," Monty said, slipping into professor mode before he caught himself. "The conditions to summon a Revenant are inextricably complicated. It's the reason Revenants are so difficult to actually—"

Me and LD just looked at him as he came to the realization that he was dangerously close to shortening his life expectancy. TK stood absolutely still, her eyes getting brighter.

The runes in the wall, floor and ceiling flared orange again.

"Perhaps," TK said, her voice measured and calm, which only added another dimension of lethality to her current state, "the reason it's so inextricably complicated has to do with the fact that Revenants are nearly impossible to stop?"

Monty nodded but remained silent.

I was considering how many seconds it would take her to blast through my dawnward in this room. I calculated at least three seconds before we were memories.

"Dear?" LD said. "We're still renovating the East Wing, remember?"

"Have you considered that the reason Revenants were locked behind the use of lost elder blood runes was because the runes were lost?" she continued, staring at Monty and ignoring LD. "Said runes are no longer accessible to curious mages that would tamper with things they do not understand."

Black and green energy crackled around her body.

Peaches whined and huddled close to my legs.

<*Why is the scary lady angry?*>

<*Monty used a rune he wasn't supposed to.*>

<*Was it her rune? Did he need to ask first?*>

<*Doesn't work like that. This was a lost rune.*>

<*Did he find it? Was it buried? No one likes it when you dig up buried things. Can he bury it again?*>

I didn't even know how to explain this one.

<*He did something he wasn't supposed to do, like when you chewed up his shoes. Remember how upset he was?*>

<*I remember. He was not happy. Does the scary lady need shoes?*>

<*No. Just stay close in case we need to get out of here fast.*>

<*The scary lady gave me meat. She is good, but scary.*>

<*Right now, she is very upset. We may need to give her some space.*>

<*Maybe if you give her meat, she will be happy again? Meat always makes me happy.*>

<*Don't think that's going to work, boy.*>

He chuffed, huddling closer to my feet as he focused on TK.

"It was not my intention—" Monty began.

LD shook his head.

"Your actions in this matter make me question the sentience of your parentage," she said, each word a dagger. "Do you realize that the blood of all the innocents this thing kills will be on your hands?"

She took a deep breath and the energy around her diminished.

"How do we stop it?" I asked, hoping to deflect the impending mage smackdown. "Not my first question, sorry. My first question is: Can we stop it? Can you explain that part first?"

"There is only one small consolation," TK said, continuing without even looking my way. "This summoning has somehow tethered the Revenant to the two of you. It won't go on a murderous rampage until it kills you both."

"That's the consolation?" I asked. "This killing machine won't go out and kill everything until it kills us first?"

"It's been dormant, but the moment you enter your plane, it will sense you," she said, turning to me. "It will hunt you down and end your lives."

"It's going to need to take a number," I said. "I have enough beings hunting me down at the moment. I currently have my own *Kill the Marked One* fan club, thanks to Kali."

"I've heard," TK said. "The Revenant takes precedence."

"In that case, I'd like to correct the order of my questions," I said as fear gripped me. "What exactly is a Revenant? Does this Revenant have a name?"

"He has a name, though I doubt it will mean anything to you," TK answered. "When he was alive, he went by Fel Sephtis."

"The necromancer?" Monty asked, surprised. "Are you certain? He was supposed to have perished centuries ago."

"Fairly certain, yes," she said. "There have been"—she glanced at LD—"tell-tale signs of his handiwork."

"Meaning?" Monty asked. "What are the indicators?"

"Shamblers," LD said, his voice dark. "They've been spotted in the city. So far no one has been attacked, but the moment you go back, I'm sure they'll be activated."

"Who exactly is Fel Sepsis?" I asked. "What is a Shambler,

and why is Monty looking like I put coffee in his tea? How is this Fel person still alive if he died centuries ago?"

"Sephtis," she corrected. "He shares a condition similar to yours."

"You mean he's been cursed with impossibly good looks and—"

"Cerebral death?" TK finished. "No, I sincerely doubt two of you could exist on the same plane."

"You know how you've been cursed alive?" LD said, putting a hand on my shoulder. "This Revenant is similar to you, except the opposite."

"This thing is immortal?"

"No—well, kind of, yes," LD admitted. "It's dead... Well, not really, more like *undead*. He's still a necromancer, though he probably relies on his Revenant abilities more than necromancy these days. The Shamblers are his minions. Think super zombies. Scary fast, magic resistant, and lethal."

"They sound like fun," I said. "You said the Revenant is an undead necromancer? So it can't die? Irony much?"

"You think this may have something to do with Strong's curse?" LD asked TK. "There are some similarities."

"Astute observation, dear," TK said, calming down further as she gave the idea thought. "It's possible this tether is tied to the both of them because of the lost elder rune *and* Simon's curse. There's no way to know without undoing York's Stormblood cast."

"That could be a bloody and fatal undertaking," LD said. "Maybe later?"

"Maybe never?" I snapped. "How about we don't undertake the bloody and fatal undoing of York's cast?"

"We'll need to do it at some point, or use a different way to dispatch the Revenant," LD said. "I think unraveling the Stormblood is the easier of the two."

"What's the other way?" I asked. "You know the one that doesn't have bloody and fatal in the description?"

"We have to hide you," LD said, "which is almost impossible now with a Stormblood bonding you. Fel Sephtis won't have a problem locating you."

"That doesn't sound promising," I said. "You're telling me a Revenant zombie is coming after us?"

"Not a zombie," TK said. "A Revenant is a different type of undead, and this one is a particularly nasty specimen."

"So a not-zombie is coming to attack us," I said. "How do we stop it? Can we stop it?"

LD nodded.

"There is a way, but it's risky."

"Riskier than facing the Revenant?"

"Close," LD said. "You're going to need another necromancer. A powerful one. One who can confront and possibly surpass his power."

"A negomancer?"

"Necro, not nego," LD said. "The only one I know is Orethe. Darling, do you know of any other necromancers who are strong enough and might want to face a Revenant?"

"Not willingly, no."

"Can't one of you unleash the necromancy?" I asked, wiggling my fingers. "It's related to being a mage, right?"

"The same way your hellhound is related to a dog," LD explained. "They look similar, but they aren't the same. We each have disciplines we follow. None of us are necromancers."

"Maybe Ezra can help?"

LD and TK looked at each other. Another unspoken conversation crossed between them.

"Hombre," LD said, his voice grim. "Ezra doesn't get involved in things like this—he's too powerful. It would be like using a nuke to take out one building in the middle of a city. You'd get the job done, but—"

"Obliterate the city in the process," I finished. "I get it. I just thought because it has to do with the undead, Ezra made sense."

"Only to you," TK said. "The rest of us wouldn't imagine reaching out to him for something like this. Tristan, do you know Orethe?"

"By reputation only," Monty answered. "I thought she retired from active practice?"

"She has," TK said. "You will have to convince her otherwise, or face the Revenant on your own."

"Are there no casts I can learn to deal with this creature?" Monty asked. "The rumors about Orethe the necromancer are far from pleasant. If even a quarter of them are true—"

"Most of them are true," LD said. "She's a nasty piece of work. She assisted the Ten on a few black ops back in the day." He shuddered at the memory. "Ruthless and borderline evil." He turned to TK. "Why didn't we make her a member of the Ten again?"

"Gratuitous use of corpses to fulfill nefarious plans, if I recall."

"Oh, right," LD said. "She tried to take over a sect by raising undead mages. Nearly pulled it off too. We had to put a stop to that."

TK nodded.

"I believe it was Tempest who convinced her that retirement was the best course of action," TK said. "It was either that or death. She chose retirement."

"No one wants to face Josephine's Stormblood," LD said, looking at us. "Which is why you may have a chance of convincing her. She'll sense *your* Stormblood."

"Won't that just convince her we need to be dead?" I

asked. "Something like that could be perceived as a threat that needs to be eliminated."

"Dead, alive, doesn't really matter to her," LD said. "She'll respect your power and the fact that you're cursed alive."

"Also the Revenant," TK said, with a short nod. "She has a brilliant mind, which means she's eternally curious. Present her with the opportunity to face a Revenant in combat, one that happens to be a necromancer, and she will be hard-pressed to deny you."

"Why *exactly* do we need her?" I asked, liking this idea less and less by the second. "Can't she just teach Monty some Revenant-erasing runes and call it a day?"

"No," LD said. "Tristan doesn't have an affinity for these runes."

TK narrowed her eyes at me.

"We are in this situation because a certain mage"—she glanced at Monty—"found it difficult to restrain his curiosity around a certain group of lost elder runes," she said. "To deal with the Revenant, you need runes particular to necromancy. Tristan can learn them, but they would be ineffective because he is *not* a necromancer. The same way you may study certain casts that will be beyond your ability to execute effectively because you are *not* a mage."

"Makes sense," I said, barely understanding the concepts. "Where does this Orethe live?"

"That's where things get difficult," LD said. "She's in a bad, bad neighborhood."

"*That's* where things get difficult?" I asked, confused. "How can going to where this necromancer lives be the difficult part?"

LD nodded.

"You're going to need to see Hades."

THREE

"Hades?" I asked, still confused. "What does he have to do with a necromancer? I mean, I get it, god of the Underworld, but this Orethe is alive, isn't she? Tell me she's alive."

"She is," TK assured me. "One of the conditions for her to remain among the living was relocation. Think of it as a reverse witness protection program for deranged necromancers. We relocated her for everyone else's safety."

"I'm not following," I said, not following. "Wait, did you say deranged?"

"Mildly deranged," LD said. "Actually, she's more like partially deranged. She's quite lucid, considering."

"Considering? Considering what? Her madness? You forced her to relocate or die."

"And you said you weren't following," LD said, patting me on the shoulder with a tight smile. "That's exactly what happened. It was really for her own safety."

"You basically imprisoned her for her own safety?"

"Not imprisoned," LD said. "She is comfortable living with Hades."

"Can she leave whenever she wants to?"

"What? No," LD answered. "That would be too dangerous."

"If she can't leave whenever she wants to, it's a prison."

"A broad and inaccurate definition," TK replied. "Can you leave whenever you want?"

"Yes," I said. "Nothing is forcing me to stay in one place."

"Really?" TK asked with a small smile. I should've known better and thought my answer through. "Then why not just leave? Why stay and face this Revenant?"

"Because we can't," I snapped. "Who is going to face him if he's coming after us? We can't let anyone become a victim because we chose to run. We don't run, ever. Unless it's a tactical retreat."

"Then, according to your definition, you live in a prison, don't you?"

I opened my mouth to respond and realized that on a deeper level she was right...and wrong.

"Point taken," I said. "We choose to stay because the consequences of running would put too many lives in danger. Like Orethe staying with Hades."

"See, dear?" LD said, glancing at TK. "He's not as dense as he appears...sometimes."

"There is hope," TK said dismissively. "*We* didn't force her. *We* brokered the deal with Hades and Persephone for her safety. A costly arrangement, but one that provided for her safety and a comfortable life, free of persecution."

"Necromancers aren't exactly considered heroes," LD added. "Even among other mages and magic users, necromancers are disliked, even hated."

"Probably has something to do with the whole 'raising the dead' thing," I said. "Most people prefer the dead to remain that way."

"That, and most of them are what would be considered

antisocial," LD said. "They seem to get along better with the dead than the living. So we made a deal for her."

"Orethe agreed to these terms?" I asked. "Willingly?"

"Others in the Ten excel at applying force when needed," TK said, a smile ghosting across her lips. A smile which chilled me to my core. "*They* persuaded her."

"Who applied the force?"

"The force was applied mostly by Josephine," LD said, slowly shaking his head. "We're actually some of the calmer members of the Ten. Some of others you haven't met are... Whew. Intense."

My mind nearly seized at the thought of LD and TK being some of the calmer members of the Ten. If they were the calm ones, I didn't think I could survive meeting the intense ones.

"What deal did you broker?" I asked, changing the subject. "With Hades, of all people?"

"I know, right?" LD said, elbowing me in the side. "It was quite a coup at the time. No one thought we could pull it off."

"Orethe would remain among the dead, living in the Underworld," TK said. "She would agree to assist Hades in any way he saw fit when it came to his duties as god of the Underworld."

"So, basically, she became an apprentice to Hades?"

"I've never thought of it that way, but now that you mention it, that's pretty much what happened," LD said. "We removed her threat from this plane and Hades got free labor. Win-win for everyone. Hades got an assistant; Orethe got to keep her life and gain knowledge."

"Did no one think making the scary necromancer an assistant to the god of the Underworld was a bad idea?" I asked, incredulous. "Didn't she become stronger?"

"Not an issue as long as she remains in the Underworld,"

TK replied. "It may, however, be something of an issue if she is to assist you with this Revenant."

I stared at her and maintained my silence, because I had grown fond of breathing, while also having all of my limbs attached to my body in perfect working order.

"So we need to go see this Orethe and convince her to stop—"

"Destroy," TK said, interrupting me. "Not stop. There is no stopping. You must destroy Fel Sephtis, preferably before he kills either of you."

"I like the 'before he kills any of us' part of the plan," I said. "What happens if he manages to pull that off?"

"That would be unacceptable," TK said. "He could enslave you, although I don't know what would happen if he killed you, Simon. Your curse would prove quite the obstacle."

"He would grow in strength," Monty said. "In your case"—he glanced at me—"it could trigger a confrontation with an angry Kali. A confrontation we want to avoid at all costs."

"Are you saying he's strong enough to face Kali?"

"What I'm saying is that Kali is not known for her pleasant disposition when it comes to you and your curse," Monty answered. "We still don't know why she upgraded your status to Marked of Kali."

I shuddered at the thought of an angry Kali confronting the necromancer and me. The collateral damage would be horrific.

"Monty, is there any way to hide or mask ourselves?" I asked. "The same way we did with Dira? Maybe go off-plane to hide our signatures?"

"Won't work in this case," LD said. "Whatever York did, it made you two a beacon to Fel. Your energy signatures are practically screaming, 'Here I am, blast me to dust.' Or something close to that effect."

"Feel much better now, thanks," I said.

"The raw truth, though painful, is better than a pretty lie," LD said. "Better to face this and die fighting this creature, than running and dying, tired and scared."

"I'm noticing both ways seem to end the same way—with us dying."

"There may be a way," TK said. "It's dangerous, but it can buy you time to convince Orethe." She glanced at LD, who nodded. "What do you think of the Ascendance?"

LD nodded then whistled low.

"We could try the Ascendance to throw Fel off their trail," LD said. "It might work. It *will* make Tristan stronger. That much I know for certain."

"Or it may kill him," TK said. "He's nowhere near an Archmage, which would be ideal. It can certainly mask them. Still, it's a considerable risk."

"True," LD agreed, "but it's not like it hasn't been done before. It can also offset the damage done by the Stormblood."

"With spectacularly fatal results," TK said with a small smile. "It can increase Tristan's power and hide them from the Revenant, at least temporarily. Scola Tower?"

"Scola will expose us as soon as we get there."

"It will also make it impossible for anything more potent than a Shambler to manifest," TK said. "We make the compromise to execute the Ascendance. A fair enough trade-off."

"Good point," LD said. "The lines are strong there."

"Is it available?"

"Last time I checked, yes," LD said. "It's going to have to be both of them, though. Won't work if we just do Tristan."

"True," TK agreed. "Raising Tristan's energy level without

adjusting Simon's would be pointless. You're right, it has to be both of them. Good call, darling."

"Your brilliance spurs me to greatness, as usual."

"Of course it does," TK said. "How could it not?"

"Huh? What?" I asked. "What do you mean, *both of them*?"

"An Ascendance is like a forced shift for a mage," TK said. "It will boost Tristan's current power level. By raising his level, we effectively hide him in plain sight."

"Fel will have to shift his point of focus to find Tristan," LD added. "It's like changing the frequency for a mage."

"For a *mage*," I said. "I can't even count how many times you have all told me I'm not a mage. Why do I need to be part of this Ascendance thing?"

"You two are bonded now," LD said, linking his hands. "The Stormblood that York pulled off... I still don't know how he did it. It connects you two in ways even I don't understand. Tristan can't do an Ascendance alone now, even if he wanted to. Unless—there is one other solution."

"Simon's not ready for that, not yet," TK said, giving me a hard look. "We don't know how it will react with his curse. The last thing *I* want to do is confront Kali. Even I have limits."

"The sooner the better," LD said. "Do you see another alternative?"

"Let's take our chances with the Ascendance. The other option is a *final* one."

"Can't we just unravel it?" I asked, feeling bad that Monty was entangled with me. "You know, untangle the Stormblood?"

"I only know one person crazy enough to even attempt that," LD answered. "That would be the same person who performed the ritual in the first place."

"York," I said, shaking my head. "He's dead."

"Allegedly," LD said, clapping me on the shoulder. "In the

meantime, before you go see Hades and recruit Orethe on a suicide mission, we will perform the Ascendance, hide you and buy you both some time. Unless we get it wrong, then you will both die horrific agonizing deaths. Well, Tristan will. You would probably come back, maybe."

"That's really encouraging," I said, my voice grim. "Do all mages take the same morale-crushing, demotivational speaking classes?"

"Be right back," LD said with a tight smile. "Need to prep for the trip."

He headed out of the room using the same corridor we had used earlier. TK stood in the center of the room with her arms crossed. She still radiated a low, seething rage, but it was less intense than when we had first arrived.

"Have you performed many of these Ascendance things?" I asked. "Just want to know what our odds are."

"I have successfully performed several Ascendancies," TK said. "The risk of death is minimal. However, if we don't perform the Ascendance, the risk of death increases substantially for each of you."

"Are you sure we can't just stay here until Fel gets bored of looking for us?" I said. "Not a fan of facing an undead necromancer, or any necromancer for that matter."

"I'm afraid not," TK said, her voice softening slightly. "While in Fordey, you are off-plane. This room is keeping you obscured from Fel, for now. Eventually, even here he would find you. There's no escaping this confrontation. It is inevitable. Some bandages are best ripped off quickly. Short-term pain for long-term healing."

"Normally I would agree with you, but this feels like short-term pain for long-term death," I said, keeping my voice respectful. "This can't be the only way."

"The catalyst was the lost elder blood rune," she said,

looking at Monty. "This is the only way now. Once we arrive at Scola Tower, Fel Sephtis will come after you both."

She left the room, leaving us alone.

"My apologies, Simon," he said. "I'm the cause of all of this. I should have never used that lost rune."

Monty had been uncharacteristically quiet this whole time. I had a feeling what was going on in his head.

"If you try and do this alone, TK will break you," I said. "Into little mage pieces. You can't undo what's been done."

"Apparently, I *can't* do this alone," Monty said. "Not any longer. For the record, that's not what I was thinking."

"You were considering finding another mage. One who was at York's level of insane with the power to match."

"I doubt such a mage exists."

"You were going to try and convince this mage to unravel the Stormblood," I said. "Then find a way to perform this Ascendance thing before confronting that Oreo necromancer and taking on Sepsis."

He stared at me for a few seconds.

"It's Orethe and Sephtis," he corrected. "Do you really not recall the names? They were mentioned mere minutes ago."

"Am I wrong?" I asked, fixing him with my glare. Easily a three on the glare-o-meter. "You were going to try and lone wolf this whole thing, weren't you?"

"Yes," he said with a sigh. "Do you understand the ramifications of what's happening here?"

"Specifically or in general?"

"Both?" Monty said, throwing up a hand. "I may have doomed us both with the use of that lost rune."

"Possibly," I said. "But we've been in worse situations and we always have each other's backs. Always. This is no different."

"I truly don't think you understand the depth of the danger we face, Simon," Monty said, looking at me. "This is not an ogre or some angry mage. A Revenant usually requires a sect of mages to destroy."

"Well, here is what I'm seeing," I said, holding up a finger. "Specifically, we—well, mostly you—need to perform an Ascendance to increase our power level, again, mostly yours, which will act as a mask for the both of us, preventing Fel Septic from finding us right away."

"Fel Sephtis, but otherwise correct, so far," he said. "That will create a window of time to locate and convince Orethe to join our cause."

"Right, and we have to do it together because of the mess York created with the Stormblood ritual he performed on us."

"I still don't understand how he integrated the lost rune in the ritual," Monty said pensively. "That would require a staggering amount of knowledge and power, as well as the intellect to create a lattice that could function without killing us in the process."

"Seems that York had the knowledge and intellect along with ample doses of insanity to pull it off," I said. "Whatever York did during the Stormblood opened whatever door was keeping Fel locked away."

"Granting him conditional freedom," Monty said. "Our death will give him complete freedom."

"Why isn't Fel after York, though?" I asked. "He was the one who performed the ritual."

"The key is the lost elder rune," Monty said. "I was the one who initially used it, not York."

"Well, that rune caused Fel to lock in on us—again, mostly you," I said. "Does that mean we need another lost rune to stop him?"

"I certainly hope not, since I only know the one."

"Then I hope this Orethe person knows how to stop a Revenant, without a lost rune," I said. "That's about all I have concerning our specific situation."

"You *are* paying attention," he said. "And in general?"

"In general, we are in what I like to call our default FUBAR setting," I said with a shrug. "Our lives are so screwed, I wouldn't recognize normal if it slapped me upside the head."

"Normal is overrated," Monty said. "What about your mangling of the names?"

"I don't follow," I said, doing my best to look innocent, before turning away. "I get the names right almost every time."

He narrowed his eyes at me.

"Of course you do," he said. "Did you catch the part about the other solution?"

I nodded.

"Can you clarify?" I asked. "What were they talking about? The option sounded dangerous."

"What LD was alluding to was you and your training," Monty said, peering at the softly pulsing runes in the walls. "He was referring to starting you on the path."

"The path?" I asked. "The path to what?"

"Mage training," he said. "He was talking about starting your mage training."

"What happened to me not being a mage?"

"Not all mages are born," Monty said. "Many are taught. It's a difficult, sometimes fatal, path, but it has been done."

"You lost me on the fatal part. Pass," I said. "I have my weapons."

I tapped Grim Whisper in its holster.

"The time will come when they may not be enough," he said. "You have the affinity to learn. Mastery is another matter entirely."

"What I have is my magic missile, thank you very much," I said, shaking my head. "Between that, my dawnward, and Ebonsoul, I'm good. Thanks, but no thanks. I don't do the finger-wiggle tango. My plate is full actually, my cup runneth over."

"I understand your position," Monty said. "You had options before the Stormblood. Now...I'm not so certain."

"What do you mean, you're not so certain?"

"Like I said," Monty said, staring at me. "Everything you now have access to may not be enough, if we face a great enough threat."

"Then...that's why I have you," I said. "*You* bring the pain and the power when I can't. You are the threat neutralizer."

"Let me clarify, everything and *everyone* you now have access to may not be enough," Monty repeated. "That includes me, and before you mention him, it includes your creature as well. He is still a puppy. I have to assume this Revenant is stronger than the three of us combined."

"How did you come to that conclusion?" I asked, glancing at my snoring hellhound. "We are a force of nature. Do you realize how powerful the three of us are?"

"I do," he said, stepping to one of the walls and tracing the symbols. "Fascinating. The runes have a permutation sequence that evolves in a span of several seconds. No two iterations are the same."

"Sounds mind-blowing," I said, glancing at the changing runes. "Can we focus on the whole 'Revenant being stronger than the three of us combined' part of the conversation?"

"Right," he said, turning to me. "In all the time we've known TK and LD, and in all the precarious situations we have faced, not once have they offered to perform an Ascendance. What does that tell you?"

"It tells me they are smart," I said. "The idea of making you stronger with your habit of casually blowing up buildings probably felt like a bad idea."

"What changed, then?" he asked. "They're offering to do so now."

"They don't want to see us zombified?"

"It goes without saying that they care," Monty said, waving my words away. "Why perform the Ascendance now?"

"Could be a few reasons: you're stronger now; we're screwed with this Stormblood tangling thing. Could be that property values have dropped? There's also that little matter about the Revenant looking to kill us?"

"All that is true with the exception of property values," Monty replied. "It's something else, something deeper. They are worried, and this Revenant—"

"Is stronger than us," I said, coming to the same conclusion. "Shit."

"Precisely," he said. "It also means they won't be the ones facing it."

"That's not exactly filling me with confidence," I said. "What are you saying? They want to make sure we can face it without them?"

"Or at least have a fighting chance."

"Well, damn," I said, glancing over to where Peaches lay snoring. "The three of us against an undead necromancer. What are our options?"

"The same as always," Monty said with a tight smile. "We see it through to the end."

"Can't we call in the cavalry? Get your uncle involved? What about the rest of the Ten?"

"No," he said, his voice firm. "TK and LD have gone to extraordinary lengths to assist us, but the Ten have incredible responsibilities on this plane. They face threats we can't imagine, on a level of power that dwarfs understanding. The mere fact that they've taken the time to helps us as they have is staggering. We are forever in their debt."

I tried to imagine what kind of power would pose a threat to TK and LD and found that Monty was right—it was beyond my understanding.

"Then it's just us three, facing off against something that wants to disintegrate us," I said. "Some may call that scary. I call it Tuesday."

He nodded.

"I could really use a good cuppa right about now."

"You think we could get some coffee at this Scola Tower place?"

"We'll find out shortly," Monty said, turning to the corridor. "They're on their way."

FOUR

TK formed a green circle on the floor of the room.

"Are you still currently being hunted?" TK asked as she gestured. "How long has it been since successors tried to replace the Marked of Kali?"

"We encountered the latest in the UK."

"Yes, the Tate Modern," she said. "I assume that was your doing?"

"Mostly Monty, as is always the case," I said. "You sure about this 'making him stronger' plan? No building will be safe."

"What makes you think they're safe now?" she asked. "Between you, Tristan, and your puppy, every building is a potential target for immediate renovation...into rubble."

"How did you hear about that?"

"You're being hunted," TK said, giving me a withering glance. "Did you think that would escape our notice? We are...the Ten."

I was just scoring all the smart points today. I should've known they would find out sooner or later. They were, after all, the Ten. Somehow, it sounded more ominous when she said it.

"If by 'replace' you mean smear me across the street into bloody, abstract Marked of Kali art, then yes, the Kill Simon Fan Club is still going strong," I admitted, looking down at the circle. "We may have stopped the recent successor, Dira. She was lethally persistent."

"You will have to deal with that at some point," TK said. Like I said, masters of the understatement. "This most recent successor followed you to England?"

"Took her a while," I said. "We lost her for a bit, but she caught up eventually. Then we dropped the Tate Modern on her."

"Never did like that building," LD said with a smile. "Didn't kill her though. Sorry."

"What?" I said in disbelief. "We dropped a *building* on her."

"How many buildings have you two dropped or renovated?" LD asked. "Yet here you stand."

"While still being inside?" I asked. "None, at least, not for long."

"Sometimes it takes more than a building."

"Two buildings?"

"*That* would be the Montague Method"—he glanced at Monty—"but no, you have to defeat her in combat. The Mark of Kali is attained by combat. Not by creative demolition."

"That's not how *I* got this wonderful mark," I said. "I think Kali just felt bored one day and decided to make my life even more interesting."

"Hard to figure out what motivates gods or goddesses," LD said. "Though Kali doesn't really do things on a whim. She's violent, but with a purpose."

"A purpose?" I said, throwing a hand in the air in frustration. "What purpose is there in sending assassins after me?"

"Keeps you on your toes," LD replied, and pointed to the large circle in the center of the room, motioning for us to enter. "You ever see the Pink Panther?"

"The what?" I asked, taken off guard by the change in topic. "Yes, the bumbling detective who eventually solves the case by accident?"

"That's the one. He used to have an assistant that would attack him every time he came home," LD said. "Kept him on his toes. Always ready."

"So you're saying this is some kind of training?" I asked. "Kali is training me to expect the unexpected by unleashing assassins on me?"

"The imminent threat of death does have a way of keeping you focused," he said. "Though how effective it would be against you, remains to be seen."

"Or she wants to see what I do with killers after me," I said. "I still have a strong feeling she's just bored, and I get to be the entertainment."

"Or she could just be bored," he echoed with a shrug. "Who knows?"

"I'd like to," I said, looking back at the circle under our feet. "Why does this circle look different?"

"Scola Tower is a place of power," TK answered. "Its location is surrounded by defensive measures that prevent teleportation unless you know the key runes."

The circle was the usual green, filled with symbols I couldn't decipher. What was new were the five, red pulsing lines, starting at the outer edge and meeting in the center of the circle, forming a pentagon where the five lines intersected.

"Is that shape important?" I asked, pointing at the pentagon. "It looks intentional."

"Yes," LD said, looking at the shape. "This is the key to where we're going. Ready to go?"

"Do I have a choice? Because that question sounds like I have a choice."

"Not really, no," LD replied, stepping into the circle next to me. "Never hurts to be polite, though."

Monty, Peaches, and finally TK joined us in the circle. With one last gesture, the circle rose off the ground, flashed red around us, and Fordey disappeared.

As the red light dimmed, the first thing I realized was that we were in the middle of an ocean. We stood on a small island built on a large, rock foundation in the middle of nowhere.

"Scola Tower," LD said, waving an arm around. "Make yourselves comfortable."

"Comfortable?" I asked, looking around the small island. "This place is desolate. Does anyone even visit this place?"

"I hear tourists enjoy visiting the island every so often," LD said, dropping a large bag on the ground. "Not much to do here except enjoy the view, unless you're a mage."

Peaches went off to explore the island. I wasn't concerned because as far as islands went, this one was so small it probably didn't show up on a map. The chances of him wandering off and getting lost were practically non-existent; it would require him to step off the edge of the island and into the sea surrounding us.

LD gave me the condensed version on the history of the island as he prepped. He spoke as he kept his focus on the various instruments he retrieved from his bag.

Turns out Scola Tower was a former defensive military building, now a ruin located off the coast of Italy in the Ligurian Sea. It sat in the Gulf of Poets, on an island so tiny you could cross it from one side to the other, in under ten minutes.

The squat, semi-destroyed tower—the condition it was in when we arrived, just to be clear—was about forty feet tall, with thick walls around twelve feet in width, some of them missing, and the rest in serious disrepair.

Each corner of the tower had a turret which probably held a cannon, now long since gone. It had once been an impressive, if tiny, fortification, but now it looked like it was crumbling under the weight of age.

From what I could see of the tower, I figured it could hold no more than eight to ten men in the whole building. Staircases led up and down to different levels, some of them missing huge sections. The island the tower sat on wasn't much larger than the tower itself. They used every square inch when they built the place.

"Cozy," I said, looking around. "Definitely getting strong vacation prison vibes. This place looks deserted."

"Because it is," Monty said. "Except for short tourist visits. There's too much ambient energy for anything to live here for long. The lines disrupt the natural rhythm of living creatures."

"Why are we here again?"

"The Ascendance requires a place of power," TK said. "This is a nexus of power that is easy to defend—unlike say, Ellis Island."

"Does that mean no coffee?"

"That means no coffee," Monty said, heading to the edge of the island. "Or tea for that matter. You can, however, enjoy the wonderful coast of Italy over there."

He pointed over one of the ruined walls.

"I'm going to double-check the place, just in case a cafe is hiding in one of these nooks and crannies," I said. "This close to Italy, coffee is a must. Not that an excuse is needed. Anytime is the perfect time for java."

"Of course."

Monty shook his head as I took off after my hellhound to investigate our surroundings. There was no coffee to be found anywhere on the island, despite being within sight of the country most known for amazing javambrosia.

"This must be some kind of special torture," I said, looking off into the distance at Italy as LD approached. "How can we be this close to the coffee capital of the world and not one coffee shop in sight?"

"This isn't a sightseeing trip," LD said, looking off at Italy as the sun set. "Nice view though."

TK had dispelled the teleportation circle and headed to the center of the tower. That's when I noticed its shape. The original structure was shaped as a pentagon. Some of the thick walls had collapsed, but the foundation remained.

I could sense the power emanating from the stones all around us. Some of the walls even gave off a subtle violet glow.

"What is this place used for?" I asked. "There is some major energy here."

"As a place of power," TK said, "it's used to cast specific powerful spells to heighten their effectiveness."

"When you say powerful spells, is that mage code for lethal?"

"Most powerful casts have a significant element of danger," TK said, gesturing while looking at LD. "Darling, please cast the mask. We don't want any early guests."

"Early guests?" I asked, concerned. "We're having guests? What kind of guests?"

"Shamblers," LD said with a frown. "Think zombies with heightened reflexes and speed. Revenants use them as minions, and they are effective. Resistant to magic and mindless, they operate on instinct and can smell energy signatures."

"Like Peaches?"

"Better," LD said, glancing at my hellhound. "Once they get your scent...you can run, but you can't hide from them. The stronger the signature, the easier they can find you."

"There's more," TK said. "Shamblers only serve one purpose. They act as siphons, draining life energy and feeding it to their Revenant, making it stronger." She paused and stared at me...hard. "Can you see how that would be a problem if they managed to swarm you?"

"Completely," I said, taken off-balance by her formidable Clint Glint. "I would be an all-you-can-eat-buffet to them, making Fel stronger. What's the fastest way to end these Shamblers?"

"Fire and decapitation usually stops them," LD said. "Movies got that much right."

"Usually?" I asked as the cold gripped the pit of my stomach. "Why usually?"

"Well, it depends," LD said as he traced symbols on the ground. "The Abominations require a little more effort."

"Abominations?" I asked, liking Scola Tower less by the second. "Which are?"

"Those are closer to zombie ogres," LD said. "Good thing they're rare. You need a really powerful Revenant to create one of those."

"Is Fel powerful enough?"

"Oh, sure," LD said with a nod as he continued to trace symbols. "But the island won't let him. Each one of these walls lines up with a ley line. Inside the tower, they create a protective matrix barrier."

I looked around the tower.

"You realize that out of the five walls that once stood, only three remain and some of those have cracks large enough to walk through?"

"It should be fine," LD assured me. "As long as they're standing, the barrier should keep us mostly safe."

"*Mostly* safe," I said, shaking my head. Mages were the masters of understating threats. "How soon before Fel knows where we are?"

"He already knows where we are," TK said. "He just can't do anything about it yet."

"When exactly *can* he do something about it?" I asked, realizing we were on a tiny island in the middle of the sea with no clear exit strategy except swimming for it. "I'd like to be ready for the party when it starts."

"Once the Ascendance begins," TK said, "he will make his move and attempt to swarm us with Shamblers. LD and I will keep them at bay until the final shape."

"Is he joining them?"

"Can't," LD said. "Not while the lines are intact. He's strong, but not that strong. Disrupting a ley line would be beyond him in his current state."

"Would it be beyond you?" I asked. "How hard is it, exactly?"

"I wouldn't try it even if I could," LD said. "The only mage I know strong or insane enough to even try something like that would be a Montague."

I turned to Monty.

"Really?" I asked. "You can disrupt a ley line?"

"He isn't referring to me," Monty answered. "At least I hope he isn't."

I turned to LD, a question on my face.

"Dex," LD said with a tight smile. "I did say insane enough. Tristan isn't that insane...yet."

"Dex is strong enough to do that?"

LD nodded.

"Not for long," he said, lowering his voice. "There's a story that he did it once, for about a minute. Every mage in the Penumbra Consortium lost their minds. Something about messing with the Thames and rerouting the lines to bypass St. Pauls. I think he was trying to make a statement."

I remembered the power of the lines under St. Pauls from my last visit. The power it would take to divert the lines there had to be off-the-charts. More and more, I was realizing the power Dex wielded.

"That's some statement," I said. "Do you know why?"

LD nodded.

"Can't tell you the details," LD said. "You should ask him. Maybe he'll share."

"What happened after he diverted the lines?"

"Elemental from the Thames had a strong conversation with him," LD said with a small chuckle. "Convinced him to restore the line."

"And the Penumbra Consortium?"

"Banned him from the country for a while," LD replied. "But it didn't stick. Dex is too strong. Banning him is like trying to ban the sun from shining. You can block it for a little while, but not forever."

"Sounds like Dex," I said. "What happens at the final shape?"

"In order to complete the Ascendance, both of you need to tap into the center ley line," TK said, waving a hand over the ground before pointing down. "Here. This is your access point."

I looked down and saw a thick beam of red energy pulsing with what looked like runes.

"Are those—?"

"Runes?" LD said, gently moving me away from the ley line. "Yes, and when the time is right, you need to tap into that power. We'll let you know when."

"By tap into, you mean—?"

"You both put your hands into that beam and absorb the

energy as it flows," LD said. "It shouldn't kill you, but if it does? You should be okay. I hope."

"What about Monty?"

"He knows how to do this," LD said, looking at Monty. "Yes?"

Monty nodded.

"I do have some experience with energy shunts, yes."

"See?" LD said. "He'll be fine. Tristan, you know how to disengage in a worst-case scenario?"

"You mean potential death?" Monty asked. "I'm familiar with the bleeding-off procedure, yes."

"Excellent," LD said. "You need to be the anchor for Simon. If you lose control—"

"The line will disintegrate us both," Monty finished. "I'm aware. I recall the procedure, though I've never practiced it on an actual line of this strength."

"You'll be fine," LD said. "You shouldn't need it, but it's best to expect the best, and prepare for the worst."

"Let's get ready," TK said. "Darling, the mask?"

"Got it," LD said, placing a hand on the ground. "Won't last longer than five, maybe six minutes. Too much interference here."

"Plenty of time."

"I'm ready then," LD said with a nod. "Say when."

"A moment," TK said, turning to Monty and me. "Once the Ascendance starts, we won't be able to stop it. The cast will run its course no matter what, unless one of you dies. Try not to die."

"We have a choice?"

"Always," she said. "Occasionally you don't see it, but there is always a choice that leads toward or away from death."

"I'll try and keep an eye out for fatal choices, then."

"Your hellhound will have to remain outside the circle,"

she said. "Make sure he understands that he cannot break the threshold."

<Hey, boy. You can't go into this circle.>

<Is it going to take you somewhere? I go where you go. You are my bondmate.>

<No, me and Monty are going to fix what York did.>

<I didn't like him. He tried to hold me away from you.>

<I know. When the cast starts, you can't go in the circle.>

<Will it hurt you? If it hurts you, I can keep you safe.>

<It won't hurt. I think. You need to keep LD and TK safe; there will be some bad-smelling creatures coming. You need to help them stop them.>

<Can I bite them?>

<Use your omega eye-beams. Don't get too close. They are undead and probably taste like rotting meat. You won't like the taste.>

<Will the scary lady make me some good meat if I keep them safe?>

<I would hope you would keep them safe even if she didn't.>

<I would. But a good job deserves a good reward. If I keep them safe, she can make me extra meat. I'm starving.>

I shook my head at his starvation comment.

<I'll speak to her after the cast is done.>

<I will keep them safe.>

<Thank you. Stand close to the scary—TK. She will be keeping Monty and me safe.>

She gestured and formed a red circle around the center ley line, inviting us in with an extended arm.

"He says he'd like some meat after this is all done, if you don't mind."

TK looked down at Peaches and nodded.

"As long as he performs admirably—and I know he will—he will receive extra portions of meat. He understands not to engage the Shamblers in close quarters?"

"I told him to use his omega beams," I replied. "Make sure you avoid them, they pack a punch."

"I'll keep that in mind," she said, looking at LD. "Mask, please."

LD released soft gray energy into the ground as a large dome formed over the entire island, cutting the sky off from view.

"We have five minutes," LD said, looking at TK. "Your turn."

"This should be mostly painless until you need to tap into the line," TK said. "Brace yourselves."

She gestured and the circle flared with red energy, washing over both Monty and me. The circle thrummed with power as it rotated, slowly at first, then faster until the symbols were a blur beneath us.

A beam of red energy shot up from under us.

FIVE

The soundless beam of red energy shot up from the circle, disappearing into the night sky above. Monty and I stood squarely in the center of the column of energy. At first, the energy beam was slightly uncomfortable, similar to the feeling of ants crawling on my skin, making me shift in discomfort.

The itchiness dissipated for a few seconds, and I breathed a sigh of relief, which was short-lived.

At some point, someone armed the ants with flaming pitchforks, which they then proceeded to jab into every part of my body.

The pain coursed through my body, setting me on fire internally. I looked down to make sure I hadn't burst into flames. Surprisingly, my body wasn't combatting the sensation, which meant that the pain I was feeling wasn't a physical threat.

This was either a mental attack or an illusion.

Or I was melting inside—it was still too early to tell.

"I thought you said….this would be…painless?" I grated, my voice loud in the sudden quiet. "This…this is not painless."

"I said *mostly* painless," TK answered without looking at me. "Now focus your mind. The pain will become exponentially worse. Prepare."

She was right.

A few seconds later, the pain went from searing me internally to immolation-level agony. Now I was certain I was on fire, but when I looked down, nothing. Not even a smolder. I looked over at Monty, who had his teeth gritted against the pain.

"Not...not physical," he said. "This...this is a mental attack, an illusion of sorts."

"The pain I'm feeling is not an illusion," I said. "Feels like I'm on fire."

"It may help to think cool thoughts."

"Cool thoughts," I scoffed. "You wield earth-shattering power and your solution is *cool thoughts*? Seriously?"

"The mind must always be more powerful than the body," he said with a grimace. "At least that has been my experience."

He looked worse than I felt.

"How are those cool thoughts working for you?"

"Poorly," he said. "An Ascendance is not supposed to be excruciating. Uncomfortable, yes." He paused to catch his breath. "Agonizing, no."

"Maybe this is an ultra Ascendance since it's the two of us," I said. "You know, a special cast because—"

"Focus," TK said, her voice cutting through the eerie silence. "In a few moments, you will tap into the line."

TK was the only one who could suggest focusing on the pain and make it sound like a promise of even more pain.

"Having a hard time focusing on anything besides the pain here."

She gave me a look that made it clear that pain and my current experience were irrelevant at the moment.

"That is not the priority at this moment."

"Right," I said, glancing down at the ley line. "Tapping into the line."

"Once you do, it will create a momentary breach," she answered. "That will be when Fel sends his Shamblers."

The pain kicked it up into gasping territory. My brain felt like it exploded one moment and melted the next. I nodded, not trusting my voice to do anything else besides scream.

"You keep your hands in the line until the Ascendance is done."

"How will...we know—?"

"You *will* know when it's done," she said, looking out into the night. "There will be no doubt as to the completion of the Ascendance."

The beam began swirling around us, turning into a raging tornado of energy, ramping up the pain several more levels. My eyes began tearing as the beam flayed my skin with agony.

I saw Monty fall to one knee and thought he'd collapsed, but I was mistaken. He was positioning himself over the central ley line. The line burst with power and TK nodded at us.

"Now," she said, her voice echoing around the island. "Both of you, tap the line."

I heard Peaches whine and then growl as Monty plunged a hand into the line. I crouched down on one knee and followed his lead, doing the same.

That's when I started to scream.

I had never felt power on this scale in my life. This was raw, uncontrolled energy. It was impossible. Tapping into this power was like asking me to stop a fifty-foot wave with my hand. It was simultaneously drawing us in and trying to fling us away. At this rate, it would rip my arm to shreds in seconds.

Monty gestured with his free hand, tracing symbols in the air. The line beneath us rippled as the power flowed into us.

"This is going...going to kill us, Monty," I managed as the red energy flowed into my arm. "Can't...can't hold on."

"Just a little longer," Monty said with a hiss. "A few more seconds."

He placed his free hand on my shoulder and traced a rune. I suddenly felt heavier, as if rooted in place. I looked down and saw I had cratered the ground under my knees.

Around us, the red energy swirled even faster, streaks of black now mixed in the red. Another, thinner beam of violet energy formed inside the energy tornado. This one swirled counter to the large red beam.

Tendrils of energy flowed from the violet beam, puncturing our arms. Energy rushed into my body and I saw Monty sag against the onslaught.

"Hold on, Monty," I said, grabbing his free arm. "You can do this."

"It's too much," he said. "The power is overwhelming. I can't...I can't disengage. We're done."

"Try again," I said as he lost consciousness, falling to the ground, his arm still in the ley line. "Get up!"

No response.

I pulled on his arm, which easily resisted my efforts. We were rooted in the beam. When I tried to remove my hand, it barely budged. I knew something had gone wrong, but I didn't know how to fix it.

I looked around, but the outer beam had grown opaque, obscuring my view. I could hear the sounds of combat, but there was no way I could pinpoint TK's or LD's location.

Diffuse energy signatures surrounded our position.

They were vague, but powerful. I figured kneeling in the midst of the energy beam had something to do with scrambling my senses.

I didn't dare call Peaches, fearing what the line would do to him. I was running out of options and fast. A dawnward would be useless in this situation. Ebonsoul was a siphon, but the last thing I needed, or wanted, was absorbing more ley line power.

That left Grim Whisper and my magic missile—I immediately dismissed Grim Whisper, which left my magic missile. I didn't think it was powerful enough to stop a ley line, but if I could interrupt it for a second, we could use that moment to get free.

I focused and pointed my free hand at the ley line beam, hoping I wasn't about to blow us all to pieces.

"*Ignis vitae*," I whispered, unleashing a violet beam at the ley line.

My beam flowed into the ley line, slowly cutting through the red beam. For a moment, it looked like it was going to work.

Then the ley line pulsed and the world went red.

SIX

It was still night when I came to.

Surprisingly, I could see more of the ocean around us when my vision cleared. That's when I noticed that out of the three walls that were standing when we arrived, two of them had been completely blown apart.

One lonely wall remained, and that one looked like it was on the verge of collapsing any second.

"He's back," LD said. "Tristan just regained consciousness too. Welcome back—you almost left the building there for a sec."

"What happened?" I asked, feeling the pulse of my heart delicately hammering a conga beat inside my head. I placed a hand on my temple, trying to manage the pain. "Ugh, my head."

The remaining wall collapsed, falling into the ocean.

"Did we do that?" I asked, realizing that what remained of the tower had been structurally compromised. The ley line beneath us had become muted. Now, it appeared as a dim red beam that coursed with power, but was barely visible. "Did we complete the Ascendance?"

"Yes," TK said. "There are, however, complications."

"Complications? What complications? Monty is stronger and we're hidden, right?"

"Yes and no," LD said, looking at me strangely. "Take off your jacket...well, what remains of it."

"Take off my—?" I said, looking down at the tattered mess of material that used to be my jacket. "What the hell?"

"Ley lines have been known to do worse," TK said, her voice somber. "Please do as he says."

"If it's any consolation," Monty said, removing his own ruined jacket, "I can completely empathize."

"This was a Piero original," I said, removing the shredded remains of my jacket. "If he finds out, he's going to be pissed."

"You have greater concerns at the moment," TK said, pointing at my arms, then looking at Monty. "You didn't disengage on time."

It wasn't a question.

"What happened?" LD asked, still looking at me with narrowed eyes. "Specifically."

"The power overcame me," Monty admitted. "I tried to divert the flow as best I could. It was too much. I believe I lost consciousness."

LD nodded and turned to me.

"What did *you* do?" LD said. "Once Tristan diverted the flow?"

I was transfixed by my arms.

All of the veins in my arms were outlined in black and violet. The violet pulsed in time with my heartbeat. The black remained constant and ominous.

Peaches stepped to my side and chuffed a few times.

<*You smell different.*>

<*Good different or bad different?*>

<*Not-you different. Something good and bad all at once. Did you eat bad meat?*>

<I haven't eaten anything.>

<That is why you smell not-you. It smells like bad meat in your stomach.>

<You can smell bad meat in my stomach? Since when?>

<I am your bondmate. I know all of your smells. Right now you smell mixed up.>

<Not exactly helping.>

<I know what can help.>

<I'm pretty sure I know your answer. Let me guess? Meat?>

<Meat fixes everything. Even bad smells.>

<I'm sure it does.>

"Simon," TK said, snapping me back to the moment. "What *exactly* did you do?"

"The only thing I could do," I said. "At first I tried pulling our arms out of the line. That didn't work."

"Lucky for you it didn't," LD said. "We'd be burying what was left of you two. You couldn't pull your arms out, then—?"

"I went through my options," I said, glancing at my forearms. "Only thing I had that wouldn't make things worse, or at least worse than it already was, was my magic missile. I thought that would divert the line long enough to pull our arms out of it. Monty wasn't looking good."

"You fired one of your 'magic missiles' into an open ley line?" TK asked. "At point-blank range?"

"Well, yes," I said, taking in our surroundings with a new perspective. "I destroyed the tower, didn't I?"

"Frankly, I'm surprised there's still an island to stand on," she said, looking around. "You used a life-force cast on a ley line. Normally, anyone else would be atomized, but you have an unlimited supply of life force."

"Why does that sound like a bad thing in this case?"

"The energy you used to attempt to disrupt the line met with resistance," she continued. "Enough resistance to cause a runic feedback."

"Is that what's happening here?" I said, extending my arms forward. "This is the effect of runic feedback?"

"No," she said, and grabbed one of my arms, pointing at the rest of the island around us before letting go. "*That* is the effect of runic feedback. Look around."

I looked around again and saw the bodies.

There must have been dozens of them, gray figures sprawled against the stones of the tower, all broken, in different states of decay.

"I...I killed them?"

"No," LD said, resting an arm on my shoulder. "They arrived that way. Those were Shamblers. Do you notice anything odd about them?"

"You're kidding, right?" I said, glancing at him. "They're all dead and decomposing. That's not odd?"

"No, look closer. Don't use your eyes."

I focused and used my inner sight. The energy washing over the island punched into my chest and I stumbled back a few steps, nearly losing my balance. LD grabbed me and held me up.

"Sorry," he continued. "Narrow your inner sight to just the Shamblers. Don't take in the entire island right now. That would fry your delicate brain."

I focused on the Shamblers. Narrowing my inner sight, I saw them covered with violet tendrils which pulsed slowly.

"They're covered in strands of violet energy," I said, stopping when it became too difficult to maintain the sight. "What is that?"

"They're inert, but they also happen to have their heads," he said. "Notice anything else? How does the air smell?"

I looked at him, wondering where this was going.

"Crisp and clean with a dash of salt?" I said. "Like standing on an island in the middle of the ocean?"

"Exactly," he said, pointing at me. "We didn't barbecue or decapitate them."

"And that's special because?"

"I'll get to that," LD said. "Okay now—slowly, a small part at a time—look at the walls of the island."

Now I really wondered if he had suffered some kind of head blow.

"Walls?" I said, pointing out the obvious. "What walls? They aren't there. Are you feeling okay?"

"Look," he said, pointing to the perimeter of the island. "Again, slowly. A little at a time. Without your eyes."

I focused on the walls, or where the walls used to be. A brilliant lattice of red energy surrounded the island in the exact place where the walls used to be. I noticed, in some places, the walls of red energy were missing sections, as if the energy was being interrupted.

"The walls of red energy? Are those the ley lines?"

"A small part of them," TK said, with a nod. "The interruptions are the issue. This place of power has been compromised. You two managed to somehow interrupt the ley lines around the island enough to disrupt the flow."

"It sounds like you're saying we broke the ley lines," I said, somewhat defensively. "That was an accident."

"I doubt anyone walking this planet has enough power to break a ley line," LD said. "No one is *that* strong."

"So we didn't break the ley line?" I asked, relieved.

"Not exactly," TK said. "Whatever you did during the Ascendance sent a blast of energy outward, destroying the Shamblers and interrupting the flow of the ley lines around this place of power."

"Why does that sound like a bad thing?" I asked. "Isn't that something any mage could do?"

"You're not a mage, Simon," TK said. "You shouldn't have been able to survive blasting the ley line. The runic feedback should have disintegrated you, but it didn't. It's why Tristan was supposed to shunt the energy to disengage, not interrupt it."

"I could do neither," Monty said. "It was too powerful."

"You may still be weakened from the effects of the Stormblood," she said. "I should have anticipated that. It still doesn't explain Simon's condition."

"Why does this sound like the first half of a dire prognosis?" I asked. "One of those: 'Well, that was amazing, too bad you're going to die in a day or three.'"

TK pointed to my arms.

"That is runic poisoning," she said, her voice grave. "There is no cure for poisoning that advanced. Not even amputation would help at this point."

"Thanks," I said, lowering my arms fast. "I'd like to keep all my limbs attached, if you don't mind."

"Honestly I don't know how we're having this conversation," TK continued. "You should, by all accounts, be writhing in agony on the ground right now as you slowly die a horrific death."

"For a second there, I was almost feeling optimistic," I said. "Thank you for destroying that illusion."

"Runic poisoning?" Monty asked. "How can that be?"

"As urgent as that may be, we have other pressing matters to attend to," TK said, turning to face the ocean. "I can't form a circle to get us off this island, not until the lines are restored to full strength."

"How long will that be?"

"At least a few hours," LD said. "But we don't have that long."

"Why? Is the island sinking or something?" I asked, looking around. "What could be more pressing than my current poisoning?"

I held up a forearm to get a better look at my poisoning.

Why isn't my body working overtime to heal this?

"He's getting closer," LD said, ignoring me. "Can we do it here?"

"A minute on the outside," TK said. "He'll be using a vessel, which works to our advantage. He won't be able to confront us directly yet."

"Who's getting closer?" I asked, looking at Monty. He returned my look and then looked off in the same direction TK was looking. "Any clue?"

"A substantial energy signature is approaching us," Monty said, peering into the night. "I don't know what it is."

"There you are," said a voice from behind us. "I look forward to your imminent demise."

I turned.

And immediately regretted it.

What I saw nearly short-circuited my brain. Standing on one of the rocky outcroppings around the island stood an enormous figure covered in black energy.

"I'm guessing that's what's more pressing than my poisoning," I said. "Abomination?"

"Worse," LD said. "Revenant using an Abomination's body."

SEVEN

TK stepped forward, green-black energy crackling around her body. She closed the gap between her and the creature standing on the group of rocks several feet away from the edge of the island.

When I focused—making sure to not do a full-blown gaze—I noticed the creature was just on the other side of the ley-line energy wall. A wave of fear threatened to squeeze me into flight mode.

This wasn't normal fear. Every cell in my body wanted to run in the opposite direction. I had experienced plenty of scary-looking creatures since stepping into the world of mages and more.

This was something else. This fear was coming *from* the creature, not because of it. It tried to compel me to run, to cower, and surrender.

TK gestured, forming a large orb of green energy and releasing it into the air above us, lighting the island. The orb was bright enough to give me a better view of the creature.

I really wished she hadn't cast that orb.

However hideous I thought ogres were, this creature,

this Abomination, had taken the ugly stick and beaten himself into a new dimension of disgusting. It was so hideous, it made ogres look positively handsome in comparison.

I felt physically ill as my stomach clenched and did a few somersaults. The name was perfect. In fact, if there was something worse than an abomination, this creature could claim that title, too. Abomination was too nice a description, it was closer to an abominathema. My brain seized as I tried and failed to focus on its face.

"Wow," I said under my breath as I regained my composure. "That's a face not even a mother could love."

"Fel Sephtis," TK said, keeping her voice even. "You have no claim here."

"The lapdog of the Morrigan," Fel-Abomination said with a sneer. "You've grown. Has the Death Bitch let you off your leash? How long has it been?"

TK cocked her head to one side and smiled in response. I looked around for shelter, but found nothing on the island that could withstand a blast from an angry TK.

I braced myself, realizing a few things in that moment.

TK had history with this Fel Sephtis. It must've been back when she worked with the Morrigan, a fact which still made me wonder. Fel was treating her like she was still the Morrigan's assassin, or cleaner, or whatever she really did for the Death Goddess.

He was either incredibly suicidal or incredibly powerful, and had no fear or respect for TK or the Morrigan.

Alone, they demanded a healthy dose of both—together, they were unimaginably powerful.

The fact that he would insult TK to her face without fear of reprisal meant that the last time he had faced her she wasn't as strong as she was now.

Acting as if that was still the case was a tactical error.

I saw LD tense as Fel insulted TK. He showed immense restraint as she nodded her head and stared at Fel.

"This *pendejo* wants me to dust his ass," LD said under his breath as he flexed the muscles of his jaw. "He's lucky the lines have screwed up the energy on the island."

"What does that mean?"

"It means we aren't at full strength," LD said.

"That doesn't sound good."

"It's not much of an issue," he said with a crooked smile. "Neither is he."

"It *has* been some time," TK said, her voice pleasant. The part of my brain that recognized danger rang all the alarms, pulled down on the steel shutters, and evacuated the building for the reinforced underground bunker. "State your purpose."

"My purpose?" Fel asked. "You know my purpose. Death and Chaos."

At the mention of the old god, my blood froze.

Is Fel an agent of Chaos?

"You no longer have a place on this plane," TK said. "Return to where you came from. You are not welcome here."

"I disagree," Fel-Abomination said. "Those two have summoned me." He pointed at Monty and me. "In particular, the young mage. He opened my door and invited me here, to *this* plane—*my* plane. It truly has been a long time." Fel-Abomination gave Monty a short bow. "Thank you."

"I did no such thing," Monty said. "I extended no invitation to you."

"Oh, but you have, young Montague," Fel-Abomination said. I noticed Monty tense at the mention of his name. "You used a lost elder blood rune. Did you understand its purpose? I think not. Your family has always been reckless and arrogant. Tell me, did they chastise you for its use? Were you properly reprimanded for the use of forbidden runes? Do they still fear *real* power?"

"You don't know me," Monty said, "or my family."

"Wrong. I know your family well," he said. "Well enough to hate each and every single Montague that is still alive. Besides, your energy signature is evident, although you have gone through great pains to obscure it. Where is Alaric? I know he must live; he's too stubborn to die before I kill him. Why is he absent?"

Fel-Abomination looked around as if searching for someone.

"Who is that?" I asked Monty. "Do you know an Alaric?"

Monty nodded.

"He has pressing matters to attend to," TK said. "Did you think your arrival would matter to him, or *anyone,* for that matter? You are insignificant."

"No matter," Fel-Abomination said. "If he is alive, I will relieve him of his miserable existence soon enough. I'm certain the demise of his family member will get his undivided attention."

"Is pissing off the Fel-Abomination a good idea?" I asked, keeping my voice low. "Do we really know an Alaric?"

"He may be annoyed, but he's not foolish," LD said. "Notice how he hasn't stepped on the island?"

I had noticed how the Fel-Abomination remained on the small outcropping that was near the island, but stayed off the island proper. It was almost as if he feared stepping on the island itself.

"Why doesn't he come closer?" I asked. "It's not like the lines can stop him, can they?"

"He's weakened in his current state, which explains using the Abomination. If he stepped on the island, the disruption of the lines would weaken him further, and he would lose control of the Abomination."

"Who's Alaric?"

"You know him as Dex," LD said. "Same person. Different names."

I looked at Monty, who nodded.

"Eyes up," LD said. "We have incoming. Shamblers."

"Incoming? From where? I don't—"

All around us, misshapen figures began to form out of dust and debris. They remained vaguely human-shaped as they came into view. Even the ones that had been inert earlier began to shift and move.

"This is your ploy?" TK said "You dispatch these mindless minions against us? You truly are pathetic."

A group of Shamblers had formed near TK. She waved a hand in their direction, unleashing a blast of green-black energy, turning them back to dust a second later.

Fel-Abomination narrowed his eyes and stared at TK.

"It would seem I have underestimated your abilities," Fel-Abomination said with a smile which turned my stomach further. "You have learned a few things. In my exile, I too, have done the same."

He extended an arm and I felt the surge of power.

"Shit," LD said, gesturing. "Heavy hitters. Brace yourself."

"Give me the mage and the..." Fel-Abomination stared at me as if noticing me for the first time. "He is cursed...by Kali, no less. Fascinating. Surrender the mage and the cursed one to me and I will leave this plane untouched. Defy me and I will kill...everything."

"You'll excuse me if I have a difficult time believing an unrepentant liar," TK answered. "The truth has never crossed your lips."

"I will have them and be free."

"If you want them, you will have to come get them," TK said. "We're right here, take them. Do you think you can?"

Fel-Abomination laughed—well, I guessed it was a laugh.

It sounded like taking a hammer to a bag filled with glass and rocks, smashing it repeatedly.

"Stupid child. You are all dead already," Fel-Abomination answered, raising his arm. Three Abominations formed on the island. These were smaller versions of the one standing off the island, but larger than the Shamblers. "You just don't realize it yet."

Fel-Abomination stepped back off the small outcropping and disappeared into the ocean. The three Abominations roared into the night as the now fully-formed Shamblers screeched. The combination of the roaring and the high-pitched screeching set my teeth on edge.

I drew Grim Whisper as Monty and LD formed orbs of power. Peaches growled by my feet and I could see his eyes begin to glow.

<*Can I bite them now?*>

<*No. They're undead and dangerous. Stomp them, but no biting, and stay away from the big ones. Can you do that?*>

<*Yes.*>

He blinked out a second later.

TK stepped back to where we stood and unleashed a cloak of power that covered her body with a deeper shield of black and green energy. The energy around her expanded, encircling us.

"That's not much of a shield, dear," LD said. "They'll see right through that. Also, feeling a bit neglected here."

"I'd never neglect you, but you don't need shielding, darling," she answered. "It's for Tristan and Simon. They are the real targets."

"Understood," LD said, with crooked smile. "I knew that."

"I have no doubt," she said, looking at Monty and me. "Take defensive positions behind us. We will deal with the threat. Simon, especially: do not allow the Shamblers near you."

"What about you two?" I asked. "What are you going to do?"

"Kill them all," TK said, her voice hard. "Again."

The Undead rushed at us.

EIGHT

I fired Grim Whisper, not trusting myself to use a magic missile in such close quarters without hitting Monty, TK, or LD.

Peaches blinked in and out of sight, stomping on the Shamblers whenever he appeared, and blinking out before an Abomination got too close.

Monty unleashed a barrage of violet orbs which crashed into a group of Shamblers, trapping them in a lattice of power before disintegrating them.

For every Shambler they destroyed, two more would appear from the dust. At this rate we would be overrun and have to jump into the ocean. I looked over the edge of the island.

That's when the idea hit me.

Peaches was blinking all over the island, which meant he still had the ability to planewalk. I didn't know if he could take everyone at once, but maybe one at a time?

I ducked behind some rubble and called him.

<*Hey, boy. I need you here next to me.*>

He appeared a moment later.

<Are you hurt? Do you need my saliva?>

As he extended his tongue, I shoved his massive head to one side, barely dodging a slobber-filled lashing.

<No. I'm good. Thanks.>

<What do you need?>

<Do you see those lights over there?> I pointed across the water to the coast of Italy. *<I need you to take everyone over there to those lights. Can you blink them over?>*

<Without asking? They will be angry. The scary lady won't make me meat if I move her across the water.>

<Can you do it?>

<Yes. It will hurt, but I can do it. I will take you first.>

<No—take TK, LD, and Monty, in that order. Once Monty is there, I need you to hit them all with your saliva. You need to make sure everyone is okay and not hurt. I'll call you, and you can take me last. Got it?>

<Yes. The scary lady, her mate and the angry man, then heal everyone with my saliva. How will you fight the bad people alone?>

<I have an idea, but I need everyone off the island to try it.>

<What if it doesn't work? The bad people will get you.>

<If it doesn't work, I'll jump in the water. You can get me from there, right?>

<I can find you anywhere. You are my bondmate.>

<Good boy. After you do this, I'll ask TK to make you extra meat.>

<Thank you. I'm starving.>

He slapped my face with his tongue so fast, I had no time to react.

<That will make you feel better.>

I wiped the slobber from my face.

<Go. Now, before it's too late.>

He rumbled and blinked away, reappearing next to TK and nudging her with his massive head. She turned at his touch and the both of them disappeared a moment later.

He blinked back in next to LD. He stomped a paw on LD's foot, causing him to wince as LD dispatched several Shamblers. A second later, both of them were gone.

Monty backed up to where I stood.

"I'm sure you have an idea of what's going on?" he asked as the Shamblers began to turn and focus on us. "They won't be able to return due to the disruption to the ley lines."

"I figured," I said, focusing on the approaching Shamblers. "I have an idea, but I can't try it with all of you on the island."

"An idea?" he asked, gripping my arm and turning me to face him. "An unproven idea? These creatures will focus on you and your life-force."

"I know," I said. "I'm counting on it."

"TK has been shielding us this whole time and that shield is now gone," he said. "Your energy signature will be a beacon to them. Are you mad?"

"I ask myself that every morning," I answered with a smile. "Then I have my javambrosia, and everything is right with the world, for at least five minutes."

"What are you planning?" Monty asked, urgency in his voice as the Shamblers and Abominations began to home in on us. "Do not do anything rash. Remember, you're not—"

"Enough with that," I snapped, cutting him off. "I know I'm not a mage, but I have power, and I'm going to use it."

Peaches reappeared next to Monty.

"I really hope you know what—"

He never got to finish his sentence.

I breathed out a breath of relief and nervousness. I smiled at the thought of Peaches applying first aid to everyone—a detail I knew he would follow to the letter, buying me time to try this insane plan.

I may not have been a mage, but I was beginning to understand the principles of magical power. I had just gone through an Ascendance ritual, which had increased that power.

I could feel it—literally—pulsing in my veins.

I was also standing in the center of a nexus of power, even though the ley lines around me were disrupted. I was not a mage; so I doubted the disruption affected me the same way it did Monty or the others.

I was the outlier. I somehow managed to exist outside the rules of mages and the rest. I was beginning to get that, and once you knew the rules, you could learn how to break them.

The Shamblers were getting closer.

I crouched down and formed Ebonsoul, using it to inscribe two of the few runes I knew into the stone. I reabsorbed my blade, stood and waited, really hoping I hadn't made a colossal error.

The three Abominations had held back behind the Shamblers, who were the real threat. I figured Abominations weren't siphons, but the Shamblers could drain my life force. I had no way of proving that theory except by paying attention to their movements.

The fact that the Shamblers replicated made them more of a threat. I didn't know if Abominations did the same thing, and if they did, I had sailed right into deep shit territory with no way out.

When the Shamblers were just out of arm's reach, I focused my energy and crouched down, placing my hand on the runes beneath me.

"*Ignis vitae!*" I screamed at the top of my lungs.

Black and violet energy erupted from my body. For a split-second, I tried to get it under control. It took me that long to realize I had made a fatal mistake.

The energy paused for a moment, then increased in power, blinding me.

NINE

I stood at the center of the island.

Well, what remained of the island.

Everything was gone except for the large pentagonal section I stood on, and a few stone staircases leading up to nowhere.

My body felt like I had done punching-bag duty with an angry ogre wearing brass knuckles. Everything ached beneath the warm rush of my curse healing me.

"Note to self: do not use magic missile after an Ascendance while standing on a nexus of power," I muttered to myself, noticing the open sea surrounding me. "No hiding this one. You broke the island."

It was the low roar that got my attention.

"That was impressive," a woman said as I turned to face her. "You very nearly managed to kill yourself. Quite a display of power. I am surprised you are still intact."

"I was thinking the same thing myself," I said, being careful not to make any sudden movements. She looked, and felt, familiar, but the lion didn't. It looked ferocious. "I'm not exactly feeling intact."

She nodded.

The woman, sitting crossed-legged on the rubble strewn remains, had an unimaginable power signature, though it wasn't overt like the fiery power of the sun or the crashing waves of the ocean.

There was a majestic calmness about her. It was like sitting at the foot of an unclimbable mountain. Her presence filled me with awe.

I didn't entirely recognize her, but I refrained from saying so, due to the enormous lion, easily twice the size of any normal lion—resting on the ground at her feet.

She wore a white robe with a large gold necklace around her neck. Her jet-black hair was adorned with golden and ivory accents. Over the center of her forehead sat a golden disc in the shape of a starburst, and in the center of the starburst sat a glowing amethyst, its violet light shining in the night.

Her wrists and ankles were covered with golden bracelets which jingled as she stroked the enormous lion's head beneath her. Her pale skin shone in the night, and her eyes... her eyes blazed with a piercing violet light, matching the jewel resting on her forehead.

"I mean no disrespect," I said, taking a few steps back in case the lion hadn't fed recently and felt like I would make a light snack, "but who are *you*, exactly?"

"Simon, I'm disappointed," she said, her voice a pleasant melody I would've sworn was interlaced with birdsong, except there were no birds on the blasted ruin that was the island. "Are you certain you don't recognize me? Look closely."

"Pass," I said, shaking my head. "Every time someone tells me to 'look closely', I lose a few brain cells. I'd like to hold onto the few I have left, no offense."

She laughed. It was infectious, and I found myself smiling for a few seconds before reality set in. I realized I was in the middle of the ocean with some being, and her monster lion, who had arrived because I blew apart an island which sat on a place of power.

For all I knew, she could've been the guardian of the tower, who was now pissed I had blown it apart. Guardians tended to react irrationally when you destroyed the locations they were supposed to be guarding—especially when they were places of power.

She must have read my expression, because she stopped laughing and nodded.

"Yes, you did destroy the island, but not the place of power," she said. "Places of power have material manifestations, but they themselves are not."

She waved a hand, and the island slowly reconstructed itself. I moved and ducked away from large pieces of stone, which weaved around me, rebuilding the island to its pre-explosion state.

"How did you—?"

"It's what I do," she said. "You *still* don't know who I am? Perhaps this will refresh your memory."

She uncrossed her legs, rising gracefully to her bare feet. Her skin slowly began to change into a deep blue, and my heart nearly stopped in my chest as she looked into my eyes.

This time, the smile she gave me had a distinct predatory edge.

I was staring at the goddess of death, time, and change, with a dash of violence for good measure. Now the familiarity made sense. Part of my brain, that part that usually kept me alive, recognized her immediately.

"Kali?" I said, barely finding my voice. "That you?"

She smiled and returned to her previous gentle, but now subtly terrifying look.

"Durga, in this incarnation," she said. "But yes"—she put

her hands together as she effortlessly sat down again—"Kali and Durga are two sides of one."

My brain was having trouble processing her presence on the island. I looked around to make sure we were alone. Not that it was any sort of consolation—being on this island with her and her lion, made me feel about as safe as a lamb in the middle of a pack of hungry wolves.

"Nice lion," I said warily. "This is a new look?"

"This is Gdon," she said, glancing down at the lion. "He represents dharma. Are you familiar with the term?"

"Somewhat," I said. "Dharma means duty, power, will, and determination?"

"Close," she said. "It has many meanings, impossible to contain in one word."

"And he's with you, because...?"

"He is my mount and companion in battle, among other things," she said. "Much like you and your hellhound."

"I don't think I could ride around on Peaches without giving people major heart attacks," I said, looking at Gdon. "I do understand the 'companion in battle' part. Peaches and I have faced a few enemies together."

She looked around the island and then gazed at me, her expression pensive.

"Were you *trying* to kill yourself?" she asked, changing the topic. "Is that why you called?"

"I don't recall making a call," I said, looking at my mark just to make sure I hadn't accidentally activated a Kali/Durga Hotline I didn't know about. "At least, I'm pretty sure I didn't. What gave you that impression?"

"You are standing in a place of power and then proceed to obliterate...I enjoy the way that word sounds, *obliterate*, yes... you proceeded to obliterate this structure."

"That wasn't intentional," I said. "I wasn't trying to get

attention. Especially not yours, no offense. I was trying to stay alive."

"I see no threat here," she said, glancing around the island. "What could threaten you, an immortal?"

"Shamblers," I said, and explained what they were. "There was also a Revenant controlling an Abomination."

"The undead should pose no threat to *your* life," she said when I was done. "The Revenant, however, cannot be underestimated. It poses a significant threat to you and this plane."

"I noticed," I said. "I just didn't expect to blow the island apart."

"You were not the only one who noticed," she said. "Your display of power gained the attention of many."

"Why does that sound like the wrong kind of attention?"

"Because it is. You are not prepared to meet those who now turn their focus to you. Not yet."

"How about not ever?" I asked. "The destruction wasn't really part of the plan. Actually, I was trying out a theory. I didn't really expect—"

"Am I mistaken? Did you not deliberately obliterate the structure on this island?"

She looked down at the stone beneath my feet where the runes were inscribed and raised an eyebrow.

"Yes, I did, but there was a good reason," I said quickly. "The Shamblers were going to siphon me and make the Revenant stronger. You said it yourself; he's a threat and—"

"Aren't there always?" she said, interrupting me. "There always seem to be *extenuating circumstances*. Do you know why I appeared to you this way?"

"To keep me on my toes?"

She paused and narrowed her eyes at me. For a second, I thought she was going to launch me into the ocean. I made a mental note not to piss off the nice Kali.

"This iteration of who I am is known as Durga, a goddess of protection, strength, motherhood and creation."

"No destruction?" I asked, feeling a bit of relief that hadn't been part of the resume. "This is the non-destructive side?"

"Of course there is destruction," she said with her scary smile. "In order to create, one must destroy. Especially when confronting evil. I appeared to you like this to show you another way."

"Another way?" I asked. "What other way?"

"Another way that does not require death and destruction."

"Weren't you the one that upgraded me from cursed to Marked?"

"Yes," she said with a nod. "*That* was to keep you on your toes. What is life without some tension to make it interesting?"

"Tension?" I asked, incredulous. "You marked me to add...*tension* to my life? Are you saying my life wasn't interesting enough, really?"

"I marked you because I was bored," she said, staring at me. "I had nothing else to do, what with being a goddess and having an abundance of free time. I decided I would mark you to make *my* life entertaining."

I recognized the words of a certain foolish individual.

"Sorry about that," I said, meaning it. "You didn't exactly explain why you put a hit squad on me, and I may have been piss—upset at that moment."

"And this Revenant, who 'put him' on you?"

"*That is* complicated," I said, shaking my head, trying to take this all in. "Monty and me—"

"No," she said, cutting me off again. "This was not your doing."

"Technically, no," I admitted. "But there was this crazy

mage named York, and then we went through this ritual which wasn't supposed to work, but he made it work; and then Verity was after us, not to mention your successors—thank you for that, by the way—and then the Stormblood bonded us, but it also woke up the Revenant, and then he had access to this plane..."

I stopped, because she was just sitting there looking at me with crossed arms, a small smile on her face. I suddenly felt like I was explaining how I broke the window to my mom when I was ten.

"That last part," she said, waving a hand in my direction. "How did the Revenant gain access to this plane? Did *you* open the door?"

"Not exactly," I said. "Like I said, it's complicated."

"Humor me," she said, somehow making the words seem like a threat and a command all at once. "Make it uncomplicated."

I took a deep breath and let it out slow, reminding myself that getting blasted to dust was not a good idea.

"Monty messed around with some runes he shouldn't have," I said, looking into the violet of her eyes. "He used the runes when we fought Mahnes."

"And this opened the door?"

"No, that was later," I said. "York performed a Stormblood ritual on us, and somehow the rune Monty used reacted to the ritual, opening the door."

"So Tristan Montague opened the door?"

"No, not really," I said. "I mean the lost rune did, yes, but *he* didn't mean to."

"Which rune did he use?"

"A lost elder blood rune. Something he wasn't supposed to be using. It wasn't intentional," I explained.

"Are you certain?"

"What are you trying to say?"

"I am merely trying to understand how you find yourself hunted by a Revenant, yet complaining to *me* about successors," she said. "Have you informed Tristan of your displeasure about being the target of a Revenant?"

"What are you talking about?"

"Wasn't he the one who used a lost elder blood rune of *sealing*?" she asked. "A rune that serves as a door? In this case, preventing a Revenant access to this plane?"

"I told you, it's complicated," I said. "Wait a second. You knew?"

"Simon. Goddess?" she said, waiting for me to get up to speed. "Of course I know. Everyone who needs to know, knows."

"Then why doesn't someone step in and close the door on this Revenant?" I asked, frustrated. "This isn't some lightweight necromancer. He was manipulating Shamblers and Abominations like puppets, and he wasn't at full strength, or even in the general vicinity."

"What would you have *someone* do?" she asked. "Banish the Revenant and save you from his attacks?"

"That would be a good start," I said. "Can't one of your god friends handle that?"

"That can't be done," she said with an air of finality. "I don't have god *friends*. None that would dare intervene on *your* behalf."

"Can't or won't?" I asked, treading carefully over the cracking thin ice that was her patience. "You're a goddess."

"Does it matter? The end result is the same. No one will interfere."

"Why not?"

"Because I will not allow it," she said. "You are the *Marked of Kali*. There is a certain weight behind that name."

"Are you saying you won't let anyone interfere to save *your* reputation?" I asked, sliding past the thin ice and into the frigid ocean of potential destruction. "Is that the reason?"

She sighed and looked off to the side, probably counting to one thousand to avoid blasting me to particles.

"Think. Do you really think *my* reputation is in jeopardy?"

"I'd have to say no," I answered, slowly. "Kali, I mean, you have the whole fearsome goddess image locked down securely. You're saying it's to establish my reputation?"

"You are not the *Marked of Durga*," she replied. "What fear could that instill in your enemies? And before you go further, you do have enemies, and powerful ones. What could the Marked of Durga do? Nurture your enemies into submission?"

"I'm not seeing any quaking when people say the Marked of Kali."

"That is because you have not embraced who you are...yet."

"Is that what the successors are for?"

"Partially," she said. "The other is to prepare you for situations like your bond-brother unleashing unspeakable evil on this plane."

"It wasn't his fault."

"It wasn't?" she asked. "Or are you refusing to face the truth?"

"What truth?"

"That, I will leave for you to discover," she said. "As for your successor *problem*, you seem to be handling it well."

"Well, we had to drop a building on Dira."

"And yet that didn't stop her."

"So I hear," I said. "Maybe we need a larger building next time."

"Violence is not always the answer, Marked One," she said with a straight face. "An *Aspis* can be used to attack, but that is not its main purpose. You must discover your main purpose."

"Once, just once, I'd like it if mages or gods and goddesses would just speak plainly," I said, frustrated, risking my life again. "Just once."

"Very well. I will speak plainly," she said as her eyes increased in intensity. "Tristan Montague has opened this door without the ability to close it again. You will either find a way to close this door or both perish in the process. This Revenant is too strong for you, despite your display earlier. Is that plain enough for you?"

I nodded.

"How did I do it?" I asked, as the wheels began to turn. "How did I manage to release that much energy?"

She smiled and rose, this time without using her feet.

"I will let you discover that on your own," she said. "I will again tell you this much: your actions here tonight have been noticed."

"Noticed? By who?"

"By beings you would prefer to hide from."

"Wonderful," I said, looking up as she floated above me. "More beings after me."

"At least you won't be bored," she said, laughing. She clapped her hands and created a portal. "And I will be entertained."

"You're really going to rub that one in, aren't you?"

"Yes. Others have died for less impertinence than you have shown me, but you are *my* Marked One," she said as the portal opened wider next to her. "Death will not visit you until it is time."

"When is that?" I asked. "Not that I'm in any rush."

"When I determine it to be so," she said. "You still have much to accomplish."

"Can you create one of those portals for me?"

"I could, yes," she said, looking at the coast. "But your hound is on his way. You will be leaving here soon enough."

She disappeared a second later. When I looked around, I noticed the lion was gone too. The sun was lightening the sky as I looked out onto the coast of Italy.

"Well, that was informative and cryptic all at once," I muttered to myself, going over her words. "Typical."

Peaches appeared next to me a few seconds later.

<Are you ready to go? They did not want my healing, but I was too strong and saved them all with my saliva. I was about to give them a second healing, but they stopped me that time.>

I smiled at the thought.

<How exactly did they stop you?>

I had an idea of the method used.

<The scary lady made me extra meat and I had to stop to eat it. I can't let the meat become bad. So I stopped the second healing to eat. They all looked much better after I treated them the first time.>

<I can imagine they were very happy to be healed by your saliva.>

<I don't think so. The angry man kept trying to push me away. But he isn't strong enough. If he ate meat he could be. Can we go now?>

<Yes. Let's go. We need to deal with this Revenant.>

<Hold on.>

He blinked out and we left Scola Island behind.

TEN

We had left one ruin and arrived in another—an ancient castle.

"Are we doing a tour of ruined sites?" I asked after we blinked in. "Where is this?"

"Castle Lerici," TK said. "This isn't a place of power, but it sits on one of the ley lines from Scola Tower. I wonder if that is one of the abilities of your hound? It's possible he planewalks by following the paths of ley lines."

"I'll ask Hades if we're going to see him," I said. "I never did get the hellhound training manual when we first bonded." I looked out over the ocean. It was an amazing blue-green as the first rays of the sun hit the water. "That is a nice view, though."

There was a sudden silence as I realized they were waiting for me to explain.

"What?" I asked, innocently. "Whatever is broken, it wasn't me."

"What did you do?" TK asked. "There was a substantial energy spike from the Tower."

I explained what I did, and LD shook his head.

"*You* are dangerous," he said with a smile. "We may even consider you for the Ten, in a few centuries, give or take."

"How did you stop it?" TK asked. "The cascade."

"Stop the what?"

"The energy was cascading out of control, and then it stopped," she said, looking out in the distance toward Scola Tower. "Even more remarkable, it reversed course. Both of these actions are beyond the scope of your capabilities."

"I know, not being a mage and all," I said with a small smile. "I don't think that was me."

"How did it happen?"

I explained about Durga's visit.

"She must have arrested the flow of energy from Simon's initial blast," Monty said, looking at me. "If she hadn't—"

"Scola Tower would have been a memory," LD said, shaking his head. "Along with Simon, the Insane."

"Don't encourage him," TK said. "He shouldn't have taken that risk. Now he's announced his position clearly to Fel and his minions."

"That was going to happen regardless, the moment they stepped off that island," LD said, raising a hand to shield his eyes and peering into the distance at Scola Tower. "Even with the Ascendance, their energy signatures are muted at best. The Stormblood bond is too strong."

"True," she said. "However, there was no need to send up a signal, announcing his location. Who knows what else he's attracted?"

"Probably a few nasties," LD said. "Things that would notice that kind of power."

"Things and creatures we do not want face in our current condition."

"What condition is that?" I asked, concerned. "What's wrong?"

"Standing in an area of disrupted ley lines impacts our

ability to cast," TK said. "It's why the Abominations were smaller and Fel avoided stepping directly on the island, even when he had the opportunity to do so."

"Didn't seem to stop the Shamblers," I said. "They were replicating."

"Shamblers are like fire-and-forget weapons," LD said. "Once summoned and active, they run on their own, trying to siphon energy from anything living in the vicinity. Easy to deal with in small numbers, lethal in large ones."

"I'd rather not run into any more of Fel's minions, darling," TK said. "I would appreciate an expedient exit."

"Good point, dear," LD said, gesturing. "I'll create the circle to Hades. We should evacuate the location posthaste."

"Shouldn't we give Hades a head's up?" I asked. "It may not be a good idea to crash in on the god of the Underworld."

"Hades—not the person, the location," LD said. "Give me a second. This is always dicey because of the seals he has on the place."

LD continued gesturing, forming a large gray circle which pulsed with green runes.

"An excellent circle, dear," TK said, narrowing her eyes and examining the symbols that moved slowly in the circle. "It looks accurate."

"Well, it will either take us to the gates of Hades or fling us to some unknown plane, stranding us forever."

"That sounds like an adventure," TK said, stepping into the circle with a small smile. "It may even be a temporal displacement. I saw you added the runes to compensate for the shifts in time."

"Hades likes to make it hard to get to his realm," LD said with a nod. "It's fifty-fifty at best."

"You have history with Fel," I said, looking at TK. "Did he work with the Morrigan?"

"Work with the Morrigan?" TK repeated. "No. Never. She

would have eliminated him long before he attained any measure of real power. No, he feared her, as most sane people do."

"Except for Dex."

"I did say *sane* people," TK answered. "Dex doesn't qualify."

"So you knew him when you were"—I measured my words carefully—"less experienced?"

"When I was weaker," TK said bluntly, "which explains his arrogance. My history with Fel goes back to my time when I worked with the Morrigan, yes. I was still learning to master my abilities. He was an accomplished necromancer by that time, and envied me."

"The Morrigan didn't often take on apprentices," LD said. "She made an exception for TK because of her potential."

"There was also the matter of my lethality," TK said matter-of-factly. "She exploited that aspect of my abilities wholeheartedly."

"We can continue this conversation elsewhere," LD said. "We need to get scarce, before Fel tries another attack. Wouldn't want Simon to blow up this place too."

"An astute point," TK said. "Can we refrain from excessive property damage in the future?"

"That wasn't the plan this time," I said, stepping into the circle after Monty. Peaches stepped in next to me and rumbled as he nudged in close. "I was testing out a theory."

"Of course you were," LD said with a wry smile. "You can share your *theory* with us later. We need to leave now."

"That reminds me," Monty said, looking at me. "The next time you're injured, I will make certain you are given the best treatment for your wounds. I may even make it saliva-free."

LD laughed and placed a hand in the center of the circle. Gray and green light flashed as we left Castle Lerici behind.

ELEVEN

The Gates of Hades were more intimidating than I was expecting.

There was one enormous gate made of metal and stone, covered in runes and symbols. The gates seemed to be the only access point along what appeared to be an infinite rune-covered stone wall stretching out to the horizon on either side of the gates.

We stood on one end of a massive bridge that spanned a lava river which acted as a sort of moat around the walls. The walls of the Underworld were easily two hundred feet high, and the heat from the lava river threatened to cook my face.

We weren't anywhere near the edge of the riverbank and I could feel the oppressive heat. I expected the smell of sulfur to fill the air, but the Gates of the Underworld were surprisingly quiet and odor-free.

There was no wailing of lost souls, and no gnashing of teeth—not that I expected to hear teeth gnashing this far from the actual gates unless said gnashing was being done by the creature on the other end of the bridge.

Across the bridge and standing in front of the gates stood

an enormous hellhound. He was easily three times larger than Peaches in battle mode. The muscles along his body rippled with power as we gazed across the span.

It was like looking at the final form of ultimate Peaches in all his indestructible glory. Not even in my worst nightmare did I want to face this creature here, in his home—or, actually, anywhere else for that matter.

This was a creature designed for destruction.

Cerberus.

"These are the gates of the Underworld?" I asked, taking in the enormous wall and imposing gates. "Hades is really sending a message."

"I believe the message is Keep Out," Monty said, looking across at Peaches' sire. "Especially with that guard."

Cerberus looked at us from across the bridge and remained where he stood. The only indication that he had seen us was the fractional increase in the glow of his eyes.

"You think he still remembers the last time we met?" I asked, keeping my voice low. "Maybe he forgot?"

"Unlikely," Monty said, matching my tone. "We made quite the impression."

"These are the outer gates," LD said. "Let us do the talking and keep your hellhound close to your side, if you want him to stay safe. At least, until Hades gets here."

"Is he going to attack?" I asked, concerned, looking at the giant-sized Cerberus. "I could always stay on this side of the bridge."

"Hades will be here shortly," TK said. "Then we can approach."

I nodded and rubbed Peaches' massive head as he rumbled next to me. Cerberus turned at the sound and fixed Peaches with a stare.

"That doesn't look friendly,' I said. "Maybe coming here was a mistake?"

"Cerberus is not your hellhound," TK said, staring at the immense creature. "He is here to ensure no one enters without authorization."

"Or leaves?"

She nodded.

"Or leaves," she added. "It is unlikely he will welcome the presence of another hellhound, even one of his own blood. Just make sure your hound stays by your side and makes no sudden movements."

<Did you hear that, boy? Stay next to me.>

<I am always next to you. You are my bondmate.>

<Your father doesn't look friendly. Don't get too close for now.>

A swirl of violet light formed in the center of the bridge. A few moments later, a woman stood there.

Persephone.

She wore a black, free-flowing dress that swirled around her in a non-existent wind. She looked the same as I remembered.

Beautiful and lethal.

She was tall, with her jet-black hair pulled back in a loose ponytail. Her expression was soft, but her piercing eyes gazed through whatever she looked at.

She had arrived ready for battle.

She made the energy signature of the creature behind her appear practically tame in comparison to the threat she exuded. I reassessed my earlier opinion, and figured I'd rather face Cerberus in battle than an angry Persephone.

She looked in our direction. Her expression and energy signature softened as she approached us. Her smile was radiant as she rubbed Peaches behind the ears.

"It is a pleasure to see you all," Persephone said, still rubbing Peaches' head. My ham of a hellhound stood absolutely still and enjoyed it all. "What brings you here?"

"Greetings, Persephone," TK said formally. "We would like an audience with your husband."

"Let's not rest on formality," Persephone said. "Please follow me. Hades is in the main house."

She turned and headed back to the violet portal. As we approached, I saw a large runic seal on the gates behind Cerberus increase in intensity.

I could've sworn I saw Cerberus take a step forward right before we entered the portal.

TWELVE

We arrived in an office about the size of Manhattan.

At the far end, behind a sequoia of a desk, stood Hades, immersed in paperwork and conversation, speaking to what appeared to be a Valkyrie dressed in black armor. Even her wings were black, and the sword attached to her back was black, and covered in a smoky dark energy.

"You ever see a Dark Valkyrie?" I asked Monty softly.

"I don't think that's a thing," Monty said. "Though this being certainly fits the description."

"It's a thing," LD said, keeping his voice low. "You don't want to face them in battle. They take elite to another level, especially with those dark blades."

I looked at the dark Valkyrie's blade, and wondered about the energy escaping from it.

"What do they do?"

"If a god or Valkyrie goes rogue," LD said, glancing at the Valkyrie, "they get called to deal with the situation."

"Like Valkyrie black ops?"

"Nightwing," Hades said, without looking up from his

desk. "Dark Valkyries, as you call them, are known as the Nightwing. This is Vi, leader of the Midnight Echelon."

"That him?" she asked, looking at me. "The immortal bonded to the hellhound?"

Hades nodded.

"Yes, his name is—"

"Strong," she said. "We know."

"I'm not surprised," Hades said. "You have your orders?"

"Yes. We're ready to move as soon as you give the word," she answered. "Grimnir, however, would like a word with you, when you have a moment."

"I will make sure to arrange a meet," Hades said. "Thank you."

I was surprised and concerned that the leader of a Valkyrie black ops group knew my name.

"Should I be concerned that she knows my name?" I asked. "She doesn't look all that friendly."

"Consider it a testament to your growing popularity in certain circles," Monty said. "Lethal, dangerous, fearsome circles."

"That's what I'm worried about. I don't want or need that kind of attention."

"I don't think you can help it at this point."

Persephone crossed the floor with us in tow.

Hades was dressed in what I could only assume was god casual. He wore a dark blue dress shirt that shimmered when the light hit it at certain angles. This was complemented by a pair of black slacks.

No tie or jacket, which surprised me, since I had only ever seen him in his multi-national CEO attire.

The office itself was on the minimalist side, with one expansive wall covered in bookcases. Opposite that wall were priceless works of art, some I even recognized. Under the art, and directly across from the bookcases sat a chestnut brown

Poltrona Frau Kennede sofa by Massaud. Between the walls, dominating the center of the floor, was the largest Persian rug I had ever seen.

In front of his desk were a handful of chairs made by Parnian, each one costing a small fortune. The desk itself was a variation on Parnian's Spiral Desk with a custom design element on the outer surface facing us.

What I had first thought was a decoration that looked like an eye, was an actual eye, that moved and focused on each of us as we stepped closer, crossing the large land mass that was the Persian.

"We have guests, my love," Persephone said as she approached. "Can you take a break?"

Hades looked up and smiled at her.

"For you, always," Hades said, nodding to the Valkyrie who raised a fist to her chest and bowed. She glanced my way for a brief second, before exiting the office. Hades turned and looked at us before sitting behind his desk. "Welcome TK, LD, Tristan, Strong, and Peaches. To what do I owe this pleasure?"

Peaches rumbled a greeting and returned his focus to Persephone, probably in the hopes of large amounts of meat.

"I found them waiting at the outer gates," Persephone said.

"Cerberus?" Hades asked. "Was there an incident?"

"Cerberus behaved," she said. "The seal is intact and he kept his word."

Hades nodded, relieved.

"That was risky," Hades said, looking at me. "Peaches cannot enter the Underworld that way. Cer would attempt to destroy him."

I shuddered at the thought of facing Cerberus to protect my hellhound. There was no way I was going to let Peaches be hurt by his father, even if meant taking a beating.

"You would have lost," Hades said, reading my expression. "By the outer gates, Cerberus is indestructible. Actually, confronting him anywhere in the Underworld is tantamount to suicide. Even I would reconsider facing him here, and I'm his bondmate."

"I'm glad it didn't come to that," I said, after a pause. "We have an issue."

Hades smiled as Persephone called to my hellhound, who padded over to where she sat. She proceeded to create a large sausage and fed it to my black hole of a hellhound.

He inhaled the meat, and then lay on his side, doing his best imitation of a bump on a log. Persephone proceeded to rub his sides as he lay at her feet, no doubt angling for another sausage.

"If you are here," Hades said, growing serious, "I'm certain it's urgent."

TK stepped forward.

"Fel Sephtis is on the plane," she said. "We need to see Orethe."

"Fel Sephtis?' Hades asked. "The necromancer? Impossible."

"Improbable," TK said, glancing at Monty and me. "Not impossible."

"Fel Sephtis was sealed behind a lost elder rune, a lost elder *blood* rune," Hades explained. "He lacked the ability to open it once sealed inside. Are you certain it's him?"

TK crossed her arms.

"In all the time you've known me, how prone am I to exaggeration?"

"A valid point," Hades conceded. "Who was insane enough to open the seal? Not to mention the power required. This was a lost rune—it would require near Archmage levels of ability to release Fel."

TK looked at Monty.

"Would you care to explain?" she asked Monty. "Or should I?"

Monty cleared his throat.

"This is partially my fault," Monty said. "I found the lost rune and began manipulating it."

"Found?" Hades asked. "Where? They're called lost runes for a reason."

"A sealed room in the Living Library."

Hades turned to TK.

"Does Ziller know of this?"

"He has been informed," TK said. "And the location of the rune is sealed...again."

Hades turned back to Monty, displeasure evident on his face.

"You found a lost rune and decided it was prudent to manipulate it?" Hades asked, the energy around him increasing, though his voice remained calm. "Which rune was it?"

"The rune of seals," Monty replied. "That was the only one I discovered."

"If you had to discover one, I rather wish it hadn't been that one," Hades answered. "That one is the key to many nightmarish scenarios being released." He turned to TK again. "Are you certain only Fel escaped?"

LD nodded.

"I checked it over with Ziller," LD said. "Only Fel managed to escape. He was the only one strong enough, using this method."

"Not exactly the best of news," Hades said, getting his energy under control. "You expect me to believe Tristan unlocked a seal holding Fel in captivity? Dexter, I could believe... Tristan not so much. No offense intended."

"None taken," Monty said with a short nod. "It wasn't I who opened the seal. I merely facilitated its opening."

Hades pinched the bridge of his nose and sighed.

"Opening a lost rune seal without the proper authorization is a capital offense," Hades said. "Which mage, possessing this power, has grown tired of living?"

"York," TK said, glancing at Monty and me. "He performed a Stormblood ritual on them both."

"The Stormblood is not a shared ritual," Hades said, staring first at Monty, then me. "It's meant for an individual. In fact, every time sharing the ability has been attempted, it resulted in catastrophic outcomes, for both the caster and the target."

"See for yourself," LD said. "They have a twinned Stormblood."

"Prepost—" Hades started, and then paused, before turning to LD. "How? This is unprecedented."

"We don't know exactly," TK said. "The best theory, aside from York being a mad genius, was that the combination of the lost rune with Simon's curse prevented their immediate demise. Completing the ritual opened the door for Fel."

"It certainly appears that way," Hades said, narrowing his eyes at Monty and me. "The bond is impossible to unravel. I wouldn't even begin to know where to start."

"Sounds like York," LD said. "Still don't know how he did it, but the lost rune is part of the key. That, and Simon's curse with an ample dose of York's madness made this possible."

"An excellent summation," TK said. "But I do believe I just said that."

"Just driving the point home," LD said. "Want to make sure we're all on the same page."

TK nodded.

"Where is York now?" Hades asked, still staring at Monty and me. "Perhaps he can be convinced to undo this. I'm beginning to see he is the only one who can."

"He's dead," I said. "The Sainsbury Wing of the National Gallery fell on him."

"The National Gallery?" Hades asked. "Are you taking your renovation skills abroad?"

"Wasn't us this time," I said. "That was all York and Cain."

"One moment," Hades said raising a finger. "How did Verity get wind of the lost rune's use?"

"The Blades were probably watching Tristan since the void vortex incident some time back," LD said. "You know how trigger happy they can be. A lost rune probably sent them over the edge."

"True," Hades said. "They are quite overzealous in their misguided role in keeping the world safe."

"Overzealous?" LD replied. "More like deluded fanatics."

"Let's put Verity to one side for a moment," Hades said. "York is not among the recently deceased."

"Are you sure?" I asked. "I mean, the entire Sainsbury Wing collapsed."

"Simon?" Monty said. "He's the god of the Underworld. If he says York is alive, then York is alive."

"Oh," I said. "I didn't realize he managed all of the deceased. I thought he only handled—"

"Worshippers?" Hades asked. "I'm not like my siblings, and I'm not related to the being you know as Ezra, although he and I speak on a regular basis, being in related fields and all."

"So you know when someone dies?"

"Yes. Even if they are not destined to the Underworld I oversee," Hades said, "I am still aware of their demise."

I tried to understand the concept and failed. I knew if I asked for further clarification, I'd get some brain-melting explanation. I figured I'd leave that one alone for another time.

"Then York is alive," I said, turning to TK. "Can we find him? Maybe he can undo this mess?"

"Alive and locatable are distinctly different states," TK

said. "He is even harder than Dex to locate when he wants to hide."

I thought back to York hiding under Lord Nelson's column without anyone knowing where he was for over a century.

"We're not going to find him unless he wants to be found."

"I'm afraid not," Hades said. "Which brings us to the purpose of your visit, Orethe."

"We need to see her," I said. "She's probably the only one who can face off against Fel Septic."

"She's certainly capable of doing so," Hades said. "The question is, will she? She's become reclusive as of late. Barely even seeing me. She likes her privacy and defends it vigorously."

"We don't have much of a choice," I said. "Whatever York did tethered us to Fel. He needs us dead to be free of the tether."

"Which will allow him to go on a murderous rampage."

"Like I said, no choice."

"There is always a choice," Hades said. "In this case, every choice you face ends badly for you, but you still have them."

"I'd like one that doesn't end in death," I said.

Hades shook his head.

"Not seeing that one," he said. "Every choice I see in this situation ends in death—for someone."

"Can we see her?" TK asked, changing the subject. "Is she available?"

"Come with me," Hades said, stepping out from behind the redwood posing as a desk. "I can take you to her, but I can't guarantee she will see you. That will depend on you. Peaches will have to wait here."

"He goes where I go," I said. "Why can't he come with?"

"Orethe is deep in the Underworld proper," Hades said.

"Cer and I have an understanding. No other hellhound enters his domain, ever. If they do, he will hunt them down and destroy them, wherever they may be. This includes Peaches. This is a sealed pact on both our parts."

"That sounds major," I said, remembering the glowing seal on the gates of Hades and then looking around the office. "So this isn't actually Hades?"

"This space is closer to Hades adjacent," Hades replied. "You are welcome to stay here with Peaches." With a glance at Persephone, he said, "I can assure you that he will receive the best care and attention any hellhound besides Cerberus can receive. He will be safe."

I glanced over at my ham of a dog milking all the rubs he could possibly get out of Persephone. She created another sausage, which he inhaled a second later. Persephone laughed at his ravenous appetite.

"Such a good boy," she said, creating another sausage. "Would you like another?"

Peaches chuffed and sat anxiously waiting for the next offering of meat. He delicately removed it from her fingers before scarfing it down.

"He will be safe here with me," Persephone said, glancing at me. "Go. I will make sure he is bathed"—she scrunched up her nose—"and well fed in your absence."

"Good luck with the bath, he's not partial to them," I said before turning to Hades. "He's fine, let's go."

THIRTEEN

Hades released power and we left the office.

"How did he do that without a circle or a gesture?" I asked Monty. "I didn't even feel the shift."

"He's in his domain—and there is the small matter of him being a god?" Monty said. "I think the latter would factor heavily in his ability to teleport us without a circle or gestures."

"Makes sense," I said, looking around. "Where are we?"

"This is Elysium," Hades said. "Orethe's home is just over that hill."

I took in the area.

We were standing in a grassy area covered with all types of flowers. Trees formed small groves separated by clear running brooks, which wound their way through the trees.

"This is Hades?" I asked, mildly shocked. "I thought it was mostly lava and torture. Lots of flame and pain. This looks like a paradise."

"It's been described as such by many," Hades said as we walked. "Elysium is located within Hades, just like Tartarus and Gehenna, among other places unknown to humans."

"Gehenna sounds familiar," I said. "That's the pain and flame neighborhood?"

"The closest approximation would be what humans understand as hell," Hades said. "Some of it is...unpleasant. Other areas in Gehenna are less so. Not everything in mythology is true. Over the course of history, humanity has tried to explain what it couldn't understand, with liberal embellishments."

"But Tartarus is bad news, right?"

Hades' expression darkened.

"I hope you never have to visit Tartarus in your lifetime," he said, and pointed. "Over there. She will be expecting us."

I saw a small cottage with a short stone fence surrounding it.

It looked barely large enough for one person. The front of the cottage was simple: a plain wooden door faced us along with a large rocking chair sitting on a stone patio.

Behind the cottage, I could see another brook and what appeared to be a large garden. Windows sat on both ends of the small home, giving it a welcoming feel.

Hades walked ahead of the group.

"Why didn't we just arrive at her house?" I asked aloud. "Wouldn't that have been easier?"

"Probably," LD said, next to me. "It's also a good way to get blasted by a powerful necromancer."

"Hades is extending a courtesy to Orethe," Monty said. "He may be the god of the Underworld, but she resides here as his guest in good standing. He honors that by announcing his presence as he approaches her home."

"Understood," I said with a nod. "Is it safe to say she sensed us as soon as we arrived?"

"Yes," TK said. "Orethe is civil, but she doesn't suffer fools gladly. Be vigilant when you speak to her, and if at all possible, be polite. Rudeness is a trigger with her."

"I remember that one mage," LD said with a wince. "What was his name again?"

"Nassar," TK answered. "He felt women were inferior and had no place learning magic. His error, besides holding that worldview, was uttering it in Orethe's presence."

"It was not pretty," LD said, shaking his head. "Talk about an out-of-body experience."

"It did change his opinion," TK said with a smile. "Even though it took decomposition and the onset of gangrene in all his major organs to do so."

"True," LD said. "Gangrene black is never a good look."

"Got it," I said, noticing the elderly woman stepping out of the cottage and approaching Hades. She could have easily been Judi Dench's twin. She was thin, wiry, and moved with the grace of a fighter. Her short, white hair shone in the light and contrasted well with the black top and jeans she wore. From what I could see, she looked fit, but age was the great equalizer.

"How old is she, exactly?" I asked.

TK turned and gave me a heart-stopping glare.

"*This* is your opening question?" she asked. "Did you just not hear what I just said about rudeness?"

"I heard," I said, raising a hand in surrender. "I'm not being rude, but if she is going to take on Fel with us, she may need to run or jump or explode something. The Shamblers aren't exactly *shambling* anywhere. They move fast and replicate. She's not going to be able to deal with them while using a walker."

TK sighed and walked ahead.

"I can't with him," she said, glancing at LD. "Keep him alive."

"What?" I asked, turning to LD. "It's an operational question. I don't want her to get hurt if she decides to help us."

"Orethe may look elderly," LD said, resting a hand on my

shoulder. "That's a choice, not a product of her age, which is considerable." He looked off in the direction of the cottage. "She could probably outrun, out-jump and out-explode you, Tristan, and your hellhound combined...on a slow day."

Hades was speaking to her and I saw her nod, motioning for him to follow as she entered the cottage. Hades looked back and motioned for us to join him.

"She doesn't look frail," I said. "But *you* just said she is elderly."

"Old doesn't mean weak," LD said. "Do you think Dex is weak, or Josephine?"

"No," I said reluctantly. "Both of them are stronger than I can imagine."

"Same with her," LD said, motioning at Orethe's cottage with his chin. "Her power is subtle. She's not going to summon a Stormblood or wield some insane axe-mace, but she's just as lethal."

"Seriously?"

LD nodded.

"She may not be on par with Dex and Josephine in terms of raw power, but she's not far behind them, either. Her mastery of necromancy is subtle. By the time her targets notice it, they're dead."

"Dead?"

"And under her control. Remember that."

I reevaluated my thoughts on Orethe.

"Maybe we should try to get her to show Monty some Fel-crushing runes and leave her here?" I said. "I'm not looking to cause mass deaths somewhere. Also, I don't want to be responsible if she breaks something."

"The only thing she's going to break is you, if you keep digging that hole with your mouth," LD said with a laugh. "She can hear you, you know."

"What? No," I said in disbelief. "From way over there?"

"Yes, even from way over there," LD said, walking ahead. "Let's not keep her waiting."

We entered the small cottage.

Any concerns I had about all of us fitting in the tiny home were dispelled the moment I stepped inside. I should've been used to this by now, but every single time I experienced a location being larger on the inside than it was on the outside, it threw me.

The interior of the cottage was mind-bogglingly immense.

Everything was laid out in a modern open floor plan, loft style. The wooden floor shone, reflecting the golden sunlight that came in through the windows.

A large living area dominated the center of the space, with a fully equipped galley kitchen off to one side. Next to the kitchen was a spacious reading area, complete with several bookcases acting as a dividing wall.

Across from the reading area, I saw a large stone section of floor with a deep red circle cut into the stone. Next to the circle, I saw what appeared to be a training area, complete with wooden dummy, punching bag, kettle bells, and an assortment of weights.

On one side of the weights and training equipment, I saw a large, square, matted space designated for sparring. Inside the square area was another circle around twenty feet in diameter. This one was drawn into the mats with an intricate design.

Inside the circle I noticed an octagon, with each side containing three lines some broken, some unbroken, extending inward to the center.

Two doors were situated on the wall off the training area. I assumed they each led to the bedroom and restroom, not seeing either in the open plan we stood in.

Hades was sitting in a comfortable chair in the reading area. He grabbed a large tome off one of the shelves and began turning pages.

"How did you get Ziller's *Practical Thanatology*?" Hades asked, still turning the pages. "I've been looking everywhere for a copy."

"It's on loan," Orethe said. "I'll ask him if he won't mind my passing it on to you."

"Please do," Hades said, resting the book on his lap. "I believe introductions are in order. TK and LD you know."

Orethe nodded.

"It has been some time, yes," she said, looking at them. "How is Josephine these days? Still irascible?"

"That will never change," TK said. "It is good to see you."

"And you," Orethe replied. "I don't get many visitors. I prefer it that way. Keeps my life simple, but it is good to see you both."

LD nodded and sat in one of the lounges in the living area.

"You were never considered social," TK said. "It seems your retirement agrees with you."

"It does," Orethe said. "Who are these two gentlemen?"

"The tall dour-looking fellow is Mage Tristan Montague," Hades said. "The one who questioned your athletic ability and overall agility is Simon Strong, the Marked of Kali."

"I meant no—" I started.

"None taken," Orethe said, waving my words away and staring at Monty. "Montague? Are you related to Dexter Montague?"

"Yes," Monty said. "He is my uncle."

Orethe smiled.

"Yes, I can see the resemblance," she said, giving Monty the once over. "Though you seem to enjoy clothing a bit more than he does. Is he still allergic to dressing properly?"

"He's making progress," Monty said.

"Is he still with Mistress Death Goth?"

Monty paused for a few seconds, taken by surprise as he raised an eyebrow.

"Do you mean the Morrigan?"

"Do you know another goddess that prefers black with black accents on a background of deeper black?" Orethe asked, still smiling. "Yes, the Morrigan."

"Yes," Monty said, composing himself. "They are still together."

"Good for them," Orethe said with a nod. "They were made for each other."

She turned to face me.

"It is a pleasure to make your acquaintance," I said. "Thank you for seeing us."

"So formal," she said. "Weren't you questioning my ability to climb a flight of stairs earlier? Something about getting into fights while wielding a walker?"

"Sorry about that."

"Sorry? What for?"

"I meant no offense," I said. "I just didn't expect you to be—"

"So old?" she asked with a smile. "Age happens to all of us. We get to choose how we deal with it. I mostly choose to ignore it—one of the perks of being a necromancer. I have an intimate relationship with death and Death."

"I was told that despite your age, you have what it takes."

"It seems my public relations team has been hard at work," she said, glancing at TK and LD. "Let me guess, they started with the Nassar story?"

I glanced over at TK and LD for help. They both conveniently had chosen that moment to admire the rest of the interior, ignoring me. Even Hades had his face buried in the book he was holding.

"Yes."

"Told you I abhor rudeness?" she asked, stepping closer. "Probably sprinkled in something about my not suffering fools gladly, too? How I'm triggered by rudeness and the like?"

"Something like that, yes," I admitted. "Are you saying it's not true?"

"Oh, it's true," she said. "Nassar was an insufferable chauvinist. A product of his time who refused to enter the twentieth century. I merely nudged him into the times we were currently living in."

"With gangrene and decomposition?"

"Some require stronger nudging than others," she answered. "Did they tell you I fully restored him?"

"They must've forgotten that part," I said, staring at LD, who had suddenly taken an oversized interest in the kitchen. "Funny how that happens."

"Memory can be a tricky thing," she said. "How we perceive reality shapes our worldview. Some see me as an dangerous and insufferable prig. I merely prefer courtesy until it's no longer an option."

"What about the rudeness?"

"I absolutely detest rudeness, but I can appreciate a frank conversation, so long as a modicum of respect is maintained."

"Sounds like a mage I know," I said, glancing at Monty. "He prefers tact and diplomacy over violence."

"A good policy. Be kind and gentle until it's time to be brutal and lethal," she said with a short nod. "Now, *Marked of Kali*"—she narrowed her eyes at me—"tell me how *that* came to be."

I explained as best I could about being cursed and then upgraded to marked. It didn't make sense to keep it from her. I had a feeling she could tell without my saying anything.

When I finished she sighed and nodded.

"Who can understand the intrigues of gods?" she asked. "The formalities are over. Who is going to tell me why I have guests today? My host," she said, glancing at Hades, "was reluctant to share."

Everyone turned to Monty, who nodded while brushing off his sleeves.

"It falls to me, it seems," Monty said. "We need your help."

"My help? Why?" she asked. "You all seem quite capable of handling anything you may encounter."

"Fel Sephtis is free," TK said. "Tristan opened the door, and now Fel wants to kill them both."

"Wants or needs to?" Orethe asked. "The distinction is important."

"Needs to, as I understand it," I said. "We're tethered to him."

"Hades?" Orethe said. "Care to enlighten us? How is that dangerous fool free to roam their plane? Did we forget the last time he roamed the earth—that little incident called the Black Plague?"

"That was him?" I asked, shocked. "He caused the Black Plague?"

"Caused?" she scoffed. "Fel was always a bit of a coward. The weak can be more dangerous than the strong. They skulk in the shadows and wait to strike when you least expect it. He used rodents and their infected fleas to increase the death toll. It was clever, devious, and the act of a coward."

"Seems ingenious," I said. "He managed to deflect the blame and attention from himself onto the rats and fleas. Everyone is looking right and he's on the left."

"You would do well to remember that about him," Orethe said. "He will never confront you directly. He uses proxies and puppets. A real necromancer would have caused the deaths directly and controlled the populace to take the country."

"Is that what you would have done?"

"If I had done it," she said, her voice holding an edge of menace, "I would have started with the Crown and worked my way down." She turned to Hades. "Why is Fel free? What happened? He was sealed behind an elder rune."

Hades nodded, closing the book he held.

"Somehow, York performed a twinned Stormblood ritual that joined Tristan and Simon. In the process, he used a lost elder rune of sealing Tristan had uncovered," Hades said. "This released Fel, and tethered him to them."

"You thought it was a good idea to use a lost elder rune?" she asked, turning to Monty. "How old are you exactly?"

"Two hundred and thirty-eight," Monty said. "Give or take a few months."

"Two hundred and thirty-eight? You're a child. I have shoes older than you," she said, scolding him. "You thought you could manipulate an elder rune? On your own? You're not even an Archmage."

"It has come to my attention that I may have underestimated the situation," Monty said, his face turning red as she dressed him down. "It was a miscalculation."

"A miscalculation that allowed a murderous, petty, vindictive Revenant to go free," she said, lowering her voice as she took a step closer to Monty. "Do you know how many he will kill to increase his power? His thirst knows no bounds."

"It was not a consideration at the time," Monty said, his voice apologetic. "There was no way I could—"

"Stop there," she said, raising a hand. "There was a way you could. You could have left the rune alone where you found it. I cannot believe Dexter didn't confine you for a few centuries for this."

She basically just suggested Monty should've been sent to his room for the use of the lost rune.

"It seems Dex is taking a 'clean up your mess' stance on this whole situation," TK said. "They are both in this together due to the Stormblood ritual. Fel is after them both to break the tether."

"That is the only consolation in this entire debacle," Orethe said. "This tether is preventing him from acting freely." She turned to face me. "What do you understand that to mean?"

"We need to stop him before he breaks the tether?"

"You need to *destroy* him before he kills you," she clarified. "There is no stopping him this time. It's been tried"—she glanced at Hades—"with less than ideal results, as you can see. Say it."

"We need to destroy him before he kills us," I said. "Is that the only way?"

"What do you propose?" she asked. "Tact and diplomacy?"

"Well, I was thinking—"

"Let me explain Fel to you," she said, raising a hand. "If I may?"

"Please," I said.

"You cannot reason with him; his mind is twisted beyond rationality. His moral compass has been destroyed. There is no good or bad, no right or wrong. All he knows and desires is power. It doesn't matter who needs to die to accomplish this. The only way to stop him is to destroy him...period. Tell me more about this tether."

"It seems to be constricting his ability," TK said. "From what I can see, it inhibits the use of his power through a combination of the Stormblood bond and the rune of sealing."

Orethe narrowed her eyes at Monty and me.

"Fascinating," she said under her breath. "If what I'm

seeing is correct, you two should, by all accounts, be dead where you stand. Yet here you are, alive. How?"

"My best theory is Simon's curse," Monty said. "Somehow it's counteracting the lethality of whatever York did."

"York always was a bit batty," Orethe said. "Brilliant, but batty. However, ultimately, I don't see what this has to do with me."

"Fel is slightly out of our league." I said, stating the obvious. "Can you help us?"

"With what, child?" Orethe asked. "You have two of the infamous Ten, the god of the Underworld, and a Mage Montague. You, yourself seem to be mostly immortal, even if it's the product of a curse. You don't need *my* help."

"None of us are necromancers," I said. "Fel is using Shamblers."

"Despicable things," Orethe said with disgust. "No self-respecting necromancer would stoop so low to use those mindless creatures."

"I don't think Fel has any respect, self or otherwise," I said. "He's using them as siphons."

"Of course he is," she said. "Fel has always been a leech of a necromancer. Too lazy to learn the proper methodologies of necromancy. At this point, he's just a glorified energy vampire."

"A powerful one."

"Power is relative," she said, looking at me. "Together, you and Tristan, is it?" Monty nodded. "You two possess enough power to stop him. What you lack is knowledge."

"We're not necromancers."

"No, you're not," she said. "And I'm retired."

"Is that a no?"

"Yes," she said. "That is a no. I'm afraid you'll have to find another necromancer foolish enough to get mixed up in all of this. I'm not the one. Thank you so much for the visit, but you've overstayed your welcome. Now, please leave my home."

LD and TK both nodded. I looked at Hades, who slowly shook his head. Even Monty had accepted her dismissal.

Orethe waved a hand and started walking away.

But I wasn't done.

FOURTEEN

"So that's it?" I asked, upset. "Things get a little uncomfortable for you and you retreat into your retirement? What are you scared of?"

TK stared poisoned flaming daggers at me. LD's jaw dropped as he turned to me. Monty coughed a few times while giving me the *we're not all immortal and willing to risk our lives* look.

Only Hades gave me a small smile and nod.

Orethe turned slowly to face me.

"What did you say?" she asked in a voice that suggested various forms of pain, followed by more pain, and finished off with large doses of agony. "What. Did. You. Say?"

The air inside the cottage became charged with energy. Everyone except Hades moved away from me and Orethe. It was a subtle shift of position, but they clearly let me know.

You dug this hole, now dig yourself out.

"Do you know how far we had to travel to get here?" I asked. "What we had to do?"

"I don't recall asking *or* caring," she said. "Your arrogance is astounding. You think you can just come *here*, to my *home*, and demand—"

"No one is demanding anything," I said, interrupting her. By now I realized I had crossed the point of no return. In for a penny, in for a pound. "We asked, politely, for your help."

Everyone except for Hades, was staring at me in various states of shock. Hades sat back and relaxed as if taking in a show. I half expected a bag of popcorn to appear in his hands. The air around Orethe had taken on a distinct violet-and-black color, leaning heavily on the black.

"And I refused," she said. "End of conversation. Why are you still here?"

"Because you need to help us," I said, standing firm. "You're the only one who can."

"Wrong," she said. "There are plenty of necromancers on your plane."

"None on Fel's level," TK said. "None that know him as you do."

"Rubbish," Orethe snapped. "What about the madman who released him? Where's York?"

"Currently indisposed," Hades said. "He is off-plane."

"Off-plane?" she said. "He's hiding...and *you* can't find him?"

"Contrary to popular thought, I'm not omniscient," Hades answered. "York is adept at hiding, even from someone with my skill."

"The answer is still no," Orethe said, turning to face me. "I have better things to do with my time than chasing down a psychotic Revenant."

I took a few steps away from the others because my next words could very possibly get me killed. I didn't want them caught in any blast Orethe might unleash.

I took a deep breath and slowly exhaled.

Monty saw my expression and shook his head, but it was too late. The words were leaving my mouth.

"So, what you're saying is: you're so frightened of Fel that you would rather hide here than face him?"

Even Hades raised an eyebrow this time. He nodded approvingly and maintained his relaxed stance.

Monty stepped in.

"What he means—" Monty began before Orethe raised a hand without looking away from me.

"He said what he meant," Orethe said, each word heavy with menace as she stared at me. "Do you speak for him?"

"I do not," Monty said. "I will not, however, allow—"

"You will not *allow*?" Orethe said, glancing at Monty. "You think *you* can allow *anything* here, in my home?"

This was sliding past bad and barreling into worse faster than my hellhound could disappear a sausage.

"Prove it," I said, raising my voice slightly and getting everyone's attention. "You say you're not scared, you say you're not too old. LD tells me you can handle anything that comes up. I call bullshit. You know what I see? I see an old woman hiding in some pseudo-paradise, who's too scared to face the world. You may scare the rest of them, but you know what I think?"

"Please," she replied as the energy around her increased. "Illuminate me."

"I think you've grown complacent," I said, backing up and heading over to the training area. "You're like one of those athletes who remembers their glory days when they were amazing. I think that's why you don't want visitors."

"I don't want visitors because all they do is aggravate and anger me. Like you're doing right now."

"You don't want to be reminded about how powerful you *used* to be as you slide into obscurity." I looked over at LD. "I was told you had what it takes. I don't believe it. Why don't you show me?"

She stared at me and smiled.

My heart did a quick two-step and tried to escape my chest. Her smile was a mix of surprise, anger, and death. My official assessment of the current situation: I was in deep shit, but it was too late now.

"How are you still alive?" she asked as she followed me. "That mouth of yours should have ended your existence long before you met me."

"First one to surrender loses," I said, stepping into the center of the matted training area floor. "I'm pretty sure you can handle a minor threat like me without your necromancy."

The matted floor felt about as soft as concrete.

"Anything else?" she asked, stepping onto the training area. "Do you have any last words?"

"Terms," I said. "If I win, you help us face off and destroy Fel."

"And when I win?"

"We leave you and your home in peace."

"Nice try," she said with a short laugh. "You call me out and expect to leave here unscathed? I don't think so. I'll accept your challenge, but I will set *my* terms, thank you. We fight until one of us can no longer continue fighting. When I win, you will receive tutelage in my discipline."

"I'm not a mage."

"I don't remember asking if you were."

"I have no real background in mystical or runic arts," I said. "I wasn't born into this world."

"Good. That means it will be excruciating for you having to learn the hard way," she said. "Do you accept my terms?"

"Kali might have some thoughts about that," I said, stalling and trying to find a loophole. "She's kind of touchy about me being *her* Marked of Kali."

"I will resolve any issue with Kali," Orethe said with a wicked smile. "She's a death goddess. We have a mutual understanding and appreciation. Besides, I'm sure she would approve of anything that makes you more lethal in her service."

She wasn't entirely wrong. The fact that Kali had unleashed assassins on me only reinforced her point. I glanced at Hades, who stared back, his face serious. He gave me a small nod.

"He can't save you," Orethe continued, catching my glance. "Your words are your own, and binding, but let it not be said I am unfair. Hades?"

"I will allow it," Hades said. "With the understanding that this is not a fight to the death. If that is clear, you can proceed."

"See?" she said, pointing to Hades. "Your trouncing has been authorized by my host."

Hades had been my only and last chance at backing out of this.

I tried tact.

"I don't think I could uphold the standard of necromancy you may be used to," I said. "I realize being a necromancer and being a mage aren't the same, and mages can be taught—"

"Is that fear I hear in your voice?" she asked. "Would you like to leave my home now? Are you running from the frail old woman?"

She had outmaneuvered me with my own argument. I should've known better. It was clear to me now that she was enjoying herself. She had let me maneuver her into this confrontation from the moment I stepped into her cottage. Once the trap was set, she sprung it, leaving me no way out but to accept.

She read my face as I came to the realization I had been outplayed.

"Don't despair," she said, looking at TK and LD. "Even the Ten had to cheat to get me here. Isn't that correct, TK?"

"That is...accurate," TK admitted. "We didn't dare enter a direct confrontation, so instead settled on subterfuge and obfuscation."

"Cheating, in other words," Orethe translated. "Which I admire. It worked, if only for a brief moment."

"All we needed was a brief moment," TK said. "It could have been worse."

"For the Ten?" Orethe asked. "Yes, it could have been much worse. Back then, I would have killed most of you and then enslaved you. Now? Not so much. I've mellowed with age."

"You knew this would happen," I said. "You knew we would end up here."

"There is always one who will fall for the bait," she said. "I had really hoped it would be TK"—she glanced at her—"but she's matured since I last saw her. Not so easy to goad as she once was. Don't feel bad; You were playing checkers, I was playing three-dimensional chess and Go simultaneously. You never had a chance. Do you accept my terms?"

"Do I have a choice?"

"Not really. We fight until one of us no longer can."

"No abilities, necromancy, or weapons," I said, resigned to the fact that as far as my ideas went, this one was a colossal disaster. "I promise to take it easy on you."

"Feel free to use any weapon you desire," she said. "If you focus, you may even last more than ten seconds."

FIFTEEN

I didn't last more than ten seconds.

At least not initially.

She stepped into the training area and remained on the outer edge of the circle.

We bowed to each other and as soon as I stood up straight I was airborne, flying back out of the circle. I landed hard on my back, all the air forced out of my lungs.

She stood in the center of the circle, looking down at me.

"You didn't focus," she said. "Again?"

I stood up, keeping my gaze focused on her. I had some training in CQC: close-quarters combat. I had never faced anyone who could move so fast. Not even Master Yat had that kind of velocity.

"I'm focused now," I said, getting my emotions under control, and stepped back into the circle, wary of any sudden movement on her part. "Again."

She nodded and stepped into a defensive stance, extending one leg forward and sliding it to the side, in front of her body. In one move, she had effectively bladed her body and positioned her open hands, palms out to defend her centerline.

It was a classic back-leaning stance, found in many martial arts. Her version was deeper than most, which meant her back leg was working twice as hard as the front. This stance also allowed her to move her front leg easily, using it to strike with speed, but lacking the power of a slower blow.

I recognized the fighting style and seriously considered surrendering right then. She must have seen the realization on my face because she nodded and smiled at me.

The smile was scarier than the stance, which she held effortlessly.

"You know this style," she said, remaining absolutely still in the stance that would have had me screaming in agony after a few seconds. Most of her weight was on her back leg while only the toes of the front leg rested lightly on the floor.

Both legs were bent and she looked like she could sit there all day. It looked impressive, but I wondered how practical it could be in a fight.

I was about to find out.

"Baguazhang," I said, thinking back to her initial strike. "Except I don't remember it being that fast, or using those kinds of back-leaning stances."

"Yes, my special variation, taught to me by Sifu Haichuan himself."

Wonderful. Baguazhang was an elusive circular fighting style, designed to take on multiple attackers. If she had created a variation, taught by the founder of the style himself, it was going to be nearly impossible to fight her.

From what I recalled, her style was designed to strike from any angle, while constantly moving in circles. If she was skilled—and judging from her stance, she was highly skilled—this was going to be like fighting smoke.

The entire style was based on the theory of balance, using

circles within circles. The best strategy was cutting off her circles, and using linear attacks she couldn't avoid.

I closed the distance on her, leading with a straight fist. She rotated effortlessly around my attack and unleashed a series of palm strikes designed to interrupt my breathing.

They worked.

Before I could catch my breath, she swept her leg low and hooked my lead foot, lifting my leg off the floor. Simultaneously, as she swept my leg, she swung an arm down on my chest, slamming me into the floor with a loud *whump*.

For the second time in less than a minute, she had introduced me violently to the floor. My body ached, but I wasn't about to surrender.

I should have surrendered.

"I'm warmed up now," I said with a groan, rolling to my feet. "I'm not going to go easy on you, despite your age."

"Your concern is touching," she said with a small laugh. "Please don't restrict yourself. I'm certain I can hold my own, despite my age."

"Remember that when I bring the pain."

She nodded, extended a hand, and motioned me forward.

I slid forward, moving fast, and unleashed a front snap kick designed to focus her attention low. I followed that up with a spear-hand aimed at her neck. Once I connected, this fight was over.

I never connected.

She raised a foot and deflected my kick to the side with the sole of her foot, causing my leg to cross my center. While my leg was still in the air, she smashed my hip with a palm strike, shoving me back while compromising my balance. My spear-hand was mid-strike as she closed the distance, snaking her hand around my arm.

Her open hand ended in my armpit. She bent low, bending me forward, before standing quickly and tossing me over her hip. I was airborne—again, before she gripped my arm, dropped her hips and swung down, introducing me to the floor, again—this time with greater force.

I heard the crack in my back as something gave under the stress of slamming into the mat. Heat flushed my body as my curse dealt with the damage. A gasp of pain escaped my lips, as I rolled to the side and away from her.

She stepped back and looked down at me.

"Will you surrender?" she asked as I slowly got to my feet. "Or shall we continue?"

"I haven't even begun," I said through gritted teeth, wincing as the curse knit the bones in my back. "That was good. No more holding back."

"I'm sorry?" she said, leaning forward slightly. "You bouncing on my floor was a demonstration of your holding back? By all means, please unleash your full attack. If you can."

She turned, waiting for me.

I wasn't clueless.

I knew she had me outclassed. Even as I was doing my best impression of a training dummy, I knew I couldn't surrender unless she forced me to. We needed her help. I had faced a small amount of Fel's power in Scola Tower and realized that if he ever broke the tether constraining him it was game over for all of us.

Especially Monty and me.

That meant I really couldn't hold back. I had a feeling she wouldn't try to kill me, but I knew this was going to enter new levels of pain...mostly for me.

I focused and let the energy flow through me. There was no way I was going to be able to face her in a straight-up fight; she was too fast, too skilled, and I was tired of bouncing on the floor.

I was going to need to adapt.

"Finally coming to your senses, I see," she said, extending an arm in my direction. "As I said earlier, if you prefer to use a weapon, feel free. It won't change the final outcome, but it will make it interesting."

I ignored her taunt as I focused on my options. I needed to close the distance to have a chance. I only had one shot at her and I needed to make it count.

I rolled forward and then slid to the side. She sidestepped my roll and circled around, ending up behind me, as I expected. I bent forward, narrowly dodging a palm strike aimed at my head and designed to launch me into a nearby wall. I extended an arm behind me, and poured energy into it.

"*Ignis vitae*," I whispered.

I was nearly touching her midsection as the magic missile exploded from my hand. The violet-and-black blast punched into her stomach—she slid back from the impact...and then she did something I thought impossible.

She caught it.

I paused, momentarily thrown off as TK's earlier exchange with her rushed back to me:

It worked, if only for a brief moment.
All we needed was a brief moment.

I had given her a brief moment. It was all the time she needed.

By the time I had recovered enough to move, I knew it was too late. Orethe, it turns out, had not caught my magic missile, but had merely moved fast enough to redirect it.

Back at me.

She turned in a tight circle and shoved both arms in my direction. The magic missile—*my* magic missile—raced at me.

The blast caught me in the chest and flung me into the nearest wall—hard. She raced over as I slammed into the wall, and before I could recover, struck me with open palms several times in the arms, legs, and the lower abdomen.

I heard the bones break with each strike as I fell to the floor, unable to breathe or move. The heat in my body ratcheted up to inferno level, but I still couldn't move.

I had lost. At least for the moment.

"According to the terms we both agreed to, a fight to incapacitation," she said, "you have lost. Do you concede?"

The pain racing through my body made it difficult to concentrate. I forced myself to focus long enough to shake my head.

"No," I said with a gasp. "I do not concede."

"You can't move. All of your limbs are broken," she said, looking down at me. "I've placed your diaphragm in stasis—which means that, in about thirty seconds, despite how hard you try to take a breath, you will lose consciousness. How do you intend on continuing?"

"This...this is...temporary," I managed as my vision began tunneling in. "Give me a few minutes and we'll...we'll keep going."

Orethe looked over at Hades.

"Is this some kind of joke?" she asked. "He can't possibly continue in his condition."

"He won't remain in that condition for long," Hades answered, pointing at me. "Look closer."

Orethe crouched down to examine me closely.

"This is extraordinary," she said in disbelief. "His body is repairing itself?"

"A part of his curse," Hades said. "He's been cursed alive."

"He would make an ideal necromancer," she said, lowering her voice. "Can you imagine? A necromancer untouched by death, without having to cross over? It's perfect."

"Perfect is not the first word that comes to mind," Hades said. "Besides, I don't think he will be a viable candidate for your necromancy. As he said, Kali may have a differing opinion."

"I'm not *stealing* her Marked One," she snapped. "I'm not insane or suicidal. I'm merely borrowing him. If anything, I'm enhancing his abilities and lethality."

"Be that as it may, the path you desire to put him on is a lengthy one. It will take twice or nearly three times as long than a mageborn to get him to the basic level."

"He agreed to the terms," she said her voice firm. "He will face the outcome. I have nothing but time, and so does he."

"Not if Fel gets to him," I heard Monty say. "Then all this will be for nothing. He will be done."

Monty, it seemed, was playing three-dimensional chess too.

"I beat him, even when he tried to cheat, which I respect," she said, glancing at me. "He agreed to the terms."

"He has not conceded," Hades said. "He is still conscious, and you still have the threat of Fel lingering over him. You said it yourself: this is too much of a mess for you to get mixed up in. Walk away."

"No," she said, the threat evident in her voice. "I will deal with Fel, but this child will learn my ways, even if it kills him...repeatedly."

Those were the words I wanted to hear—well, not the ones about me dying repeatedly or learning her ways, but the ones where she took on Fel. I stopped fighting against the overwhelming crushing weight of darkness that surrounded me.

"I'm going to say that blacking out in the middle of a fight constitutes conceding," she continued, looking at me again. "Any moment now."

"I'm not...not blacking out," I said, trying to raise a broken arm. "I'm fine."

Those were my last words before the world went black.

SIXTEEN

I woke up in a strange bedroom.

A few moments later, Monty walked in. The bedroom was a modern layout with a king-sized bed and state-of-the-art technology. An enormous flat screen TV hung on the wall opposite the bed.

To the right of the bed, I saw a computer station with a three-foot-wide monitor. The desk the computer sat on was a minimalist affair—sturdy, but no frills. Chairs were placed around the room: one in front of the computer desk, and another next to a large dresser that dominated the other wall opposite the bed.

I slowly stretched my arms and legs. Pain reached out and crushed me in its embrace, nearly stealing my breath before subsiding. My arms and legs functioned, but the stiffness kept me from making any sudden movements.

The black veins in my arms were more noticeable.

That can't be good.

I made sure the sheet I lay under covered them. I flexed my fingers, but felt nothing out of the ordinary.

My breathing had returned to normal, but I was going to

need a defense against that diaphragm attack. Being cursed alive was pointless if I could be taken out of commission with one attack.

"Where am I?" I asked as Monty stepped closer. "Are we still in Orethe's—?"

"Yes," Monty said, looking around. "Apparently, her home is quite spacious. She has truly mastered the manipulation of time and relative dimensions in space. I hear there is an entire lower level to her home, aside from this guest bedroom."

"Guest bedroom?" I said, looking around. "How large is the master bedroom?"

"Would you like me to inquire?" he asked, raising an eyebrow. "I'm sure she would be willing to give you a tour."

"On second thought, forget I asked," I said. "Don't want to give her any strange ideas."

"A wise choice, unlike most of the time you've spent in her presence."

"You say that like I had a choice," I said, sitting up gingerly and regretting it immediately. My abdomen felt like a large elephant had been gently tap-dancing on it. Everything ached. "I didn't see anyone else trying to stop her."

"Astute observation," he said. "Did you stop to consider why?"

"Hades can't get involved in something like this," I guessed. "He probably has a few dozen world-ending situations juggling in the air that require his immediate attention."

"True," Monty said, pulling up a chair. "As ruler of the Underworld, one can assume he is quite busy. His meeting with that Nightwing, Vi, raises more questions than answers."

"Also, you ever hear of a Grimnir related to the Valkyries?" I asked. "That sounded serious."

"If I'm not mistaken, Grimnir would be the father of the Norse Pantheon."

"You're talking about O—"

"Let's not," Monty said quickly, raising a hand. "He has a very reliable surveillance and intelligence system in those ravens of his."

"Good point," I said. "So that kind of explains Hades."

"What of TK and LD?"

"You already said TK and LD have other responsibilities. Besides, we wouldn't have been able to find Orethe without them," I said. "We can't ask them to do more."

"Well, you could certainly ask," Monty said. "The answer will most likely be no. Especially after your performance earlier."

"My *performance* pales in comparison to some of the things they've done," I said with a small grunt as I shifted position. "My performance was—"

"Reckless? Ill-advised? Doomed to fail?"

"Necessary," I said. "One of us had to do it."

"I see," he said. "You self-selected. How selfless of you. Did you wonder why you were the only one who had volunteered to be the sacrificial lamb?"

"Hades I can guess," I said. "TK and LD are a little harder to figure out. They know what's at stake."

"So does Hades. Yet they opted to remain neutral."

"It can't be because they're scared," I said. "TK and LD easily handled the Shamblers and Abominations, and Hades is, well, Hades."

"True. There is a deeper reason, and fear is not part of it."

"It's our mess and we have to be able to deal with the fallout?" I asked. "Isn't that kind of harsh?"

"Some may view it that way," Monty said, "but that is the way mages function within the world. We don't attempt to solve every problem, especially those not of our making. That is an efficient way to make enemies and race to an a early death."

"But they know what happens if Fel breaks the tether," I said. "It affects them too."

"Which is why they've helped us to the extent they have," Monty said. "I doubt their involvement will continue past this point, but they will be aware of our actions."

"So they're not going to swoop in and save the day?"

"Do you really want them to?"

"No," I said, after giving it some thought. "We can't keep relying on outside help."

"True," he said. "It has come to my attention that we are facing considerably difficult enemies. We need to, at the very least, figure this Stormblood out."

"Or you could just shift to Archmage."

"Of course," Monty said, giving me a look. "Why didn't I think of that? Let me just snap my fingers and shift. It completely escaped my mind."

"No need to be a snot about it," I said. "I know it's not that easy."

"As beneficial as it sounds, my being an Archmage would hinder my actions, rather than allowing me to act freely. Power on that level has a tendency to get noticed."

"Your Archmaginess would attract worse enemies?"

"Similar to your being the Marked of Kali, on an exponentially larger scale," he said. "Are you dissatisfied with the level of danger we are currently facing?"

"No, I just don't think your being an Archmage could be worse than being the Marked of Kali," I said. "At least we'd have the firepower to face these maniacs, like Fel, without help."

"There is always something or someone more powerful," he replied. "The answer isn't always more power."

"More power certainly helps," I said. "I mean, how much worse is it going to get?"

"You mean worse than Chaos and his assorted agents

coming after us?" he asked. "I think we're approaching the pinnacle of, 'How much worse it could get?' once old gods are hunting us."

"Good point. Why is Orethe helping us?" I asked. "She *is* helping us, right? I didn't imagine that part because my brain was low on oxygen?"

"Yes, she is. I would assume she's helping us because of you."

"Me?" I asked. " What does that mean? Did you tell her about Chi?"

"Your humility knows no bounds," Monty said, shaking his head. "She is not enamored with you. What she sees is your potential to be her legacy."

"Her legacy? If I'm not a mage, I'm even further away from being a necromancer," I said. "I don't see myself dealing with zombies and hordes of undead."

"Nor do I," Monty said. "Fortunately for you, Orethe is a specific type of necromancer. She deals in Death Magic."

"How does that make me fortunate exactly?" I asked. "She sounds evil, is what she sounds like. Death magic sounds *exactly* like zombies and hordes of the undead. What am I missing?"

"Her expression of necromancy is not focused on bringing the dead back to life, though I'm certain she has that capability," he said, entering lecture mode. "Rather, she has a distinct feature to her skill. You recall she wasn't worried about you using a weapon?"

"Even asked me to wield one—twice," I said. "Can't say I didn't think about it."

"Why didn't you?" he asked. "Ebonsoul was readily available to you."

"Ebonsoul is a siphon," I said. "Last thing I wanted was to siphon energy from her."

"Provided you could cut her with your weapon, that is."

"That was the other reason," I said, thinking about her skill level. "There was a good chance she might've used it against me. I've never seen anyone redirect a magic missile like she did. She's too fast."

"In any case, it's a good thing you didn't form your weapon," Monty said. "She could have killed it."

"Excuse me? Ebonsoul isn't alive."

"No? Consider that it's part of the same blade Grey wields. A blade which is sentient and home to a goddess."

"Shit I hadn't thought of that. But still, how do you kill a blade?"

"Orethe's ability can also affect non-organic matter," Monty said. "It's actually quite intriguing. She can—"

"Don't Spockify it," I said. "What do you mean, she can affect non-organic matter?"

"I was just getting to that," he said. "She can destroy a weapon, or pretty much anything non-organic, with a touch. She accelerates the aging process to the point of structural failure."

"Any weapon?"

"*Anything*," he corrected. "Including organic matter, of course. She broke your bones not by applying force, but by weakening their internal structure."

"What? How?"

"The same way bones become brittle due to old age," he said. "She merely accelerated the aging process in your bones —with a touch."

"How is she still alive?" I asked. "An ability like that must paint a huge target on your back."

"It was why she was considered for the Ten in the first place," Monty said. "Then she was deemed too dangerous."

"*That's* why she's down here," I said. "She can't really destroy anything in Hades."

"I'm sure she could, if she really tried, but it would prove to be futile. This domain is beyond her level of power and would restore itself almost immediately."

"This is the one place where she's not a threat," I said, thinking it over. "She must feel—"

"Normal," Orethe said as she entered the room. "It's the one place I don't have to keep my power in check all the time. I can even grow a garden."

She still wore the black top and black jeans. She padded over to one of the other chairs, turning it around and resting her arms on the back as she sat. Her bare feet curled around the legs of the chair as she looked at me.

"Thank you for the guest bedroom," I said, sitting up straighter with a wince. "It's comfortable."

"No one ever uses it," she said. "As you can imagine, I don't get many guests here." She looked around the room. "I created it because I was bored."

"I hear there's a lower level too," I said. "More bored construction?"

"No, I designed the lower level for practice," she said. "You'll see it, soon enough."

"That doesn't sound inviting at all," I said. "I've never met a pure necromancer."

"Not true," she said. "You've met Azrael. He's stronger than I will ever be."

"You mean Ezra?"

She nodded.

"Nothing can withstand his power, hence the title—"

"Angel of Death?"

"It's a little dramatic, but it's an accurate description of who and what he is," she said. "I don't possess a tenth of his power."

"Then you're the second pure necromancer I've met."

"I've never met a cursed immortal," she continued.

"You're the first. Every aspect of my life has been centered around death or dying, and here you are, cursed alive."

"Not by choice," I said. "Kali was feeling generous that day."

"Some would say that your curse is worse than anything else she could have done to you," she said. "Enough time passes, and even an immortal longs for death."

"Thank you for that uplifting thought," I said, staring at her in disbelief. At this point, I was just going to accept that everyone who wielded power was trained in the art of Demoralizing Comments. "Makes me feel warm all over."

"You're welcome," she said. "Better you learn that truth now."

"Are you really going to help us?" I asked, ignoring her descent into death topics and glancing at Monty. "Are you sure you just can't show him some necrorunes and we can call it a day?"

"Yes. I'm going to help you both, though you may not be pleased with my form of help," she said. "Also, there are no such things as necrorunes. Necromancers are not mages. If I had to give us a classification, we'd be closer to witches and wizards."

I glanced at Monty at the mention of the W word. He kept his face impassive, but tugged on his sleeve, before removing the non-existent dust, clearly displeased.

"Why would you study necromancy?" I asked, curious. "It's—"

"Evil?" she asked. "Perverse?"

"Gross," I countered. "You enjoy dealing with dead things?"

"Everything dies, sooner or later."

"I'm sure you would be the hit of any social event, but seriously, is it only dealing with dead things with a side of death, finished off with the gross?"

"I've never heard it described as *gross* before," she said, looking at me. "You don't think it's evil?"

"I consider that the *person* can be evil." Her expression darkened. "If you're using your power to hurt innocents and kill people for no reason, except to gain power? Then, yes, it becomes evil. I don't think I could ever learn necromancy."

I noticed Monty nod as I gave my answer. We had discussed this many times regarding magic and power. I still believed some magic could be inherently evil, but ultimately energy and power were tools. How they were used mattered more than their intended use.

"Why?" she asked. "Do you think it's impossible?"

"Not impossible, just improbable, especially for me."

"Can you elaborate?"

"It takes all my focus to create a magic missile or a dawnward," I said. "That's about the extent of my magical arsenal. Learning to mess with energy and death? That sounds way beyond my level of skill, and a perfect recipe for disaster on a massive scale."

"My discipline has a very unique method of instruction," she said. "I can impart most of the knowledge directly to you."

"Excuse me?" I asked, confused. "I'm not a fan of having anything directly imparted to me. I have enough imparted things floating around inside of me, thanks."

"The knowledge will be gated according to your level of power, giving you access only when you are ready to wield it," she said. "Still, it makes instruction easier for the both of us if the information is within you."

Monty rubbed his chin, meaning he was deep into professor mode.

"It *is* possible," Monty said. "There is precedent for such a sharing of knowledge among wizards, but he would need a focus."

"Mages aren't fans of wizards and focuses," I said. "I know one"—I glanced at Monty—"who gets triggered when he's mistaken for a wizard."

"Mages are, for the most part, taught that bias," she said. "They are raised in sects with a narrow view of energy use. Most fail to realize that they are similar to wizards, in that they both use a focus."

"We do not," Monty said. "I have never used a focus in my entire—"

"Mages," she said, "forget that the body can be a focus. Wizards prefer an external focus; mages prefer to use an internal one. Same thing, different method."

Monty had grown silent, rubbing his chin again. He was actually giving the theory thought, which was unlike him.

"In light of our recent experiences, I will withhold my final determination on this topic until I have more data."

"Very atypical for a mage," she said.

"That doesn't change the fact that Simon would need a focus," Monty said. "He has no training as a mage *or* necromancer."

"He has a focus," she said, pointing at my chest. "The weapon he holds within is a perfect receptacle. A seraphic siphon is ideal, don't you think?" She turned to me. "Do you encounter many demons?"

"Not really," I said, surprised she knew what Ebonsoul was. "How did you—?"

"Yes," Monty said. "How exactly did you know about the weapon?"

"My innersight is distinct from that of mages," she said. "Think of it as being able to see in a different spectrum of light."

"Like seeing in both ultraviolet and infrared?"

"A simple example, but yes, exactly that. I can see different forms of energy. Your Ebonsoul is quite distinct for those who can see. Your bond to it would make it the perfect focus for your training."

"Wouldn't it be easier to give me a book?" I asked. "Doesn't matter how thick it is. I would study it, really."

"You are a strange individual, Simon Strong," she said, looking down at my arms. "How long ago were you poisoned?"

I looked down, but my arms were still covered by the sheet I lay under.

"Ever since the Ascendance ritual," I said. "How did you know?"

"When I hit you, I felt the presence of the poison in your body," she said. "It felt like runic poisoning, but I have never felt any poisoning this advanced without the target being deceased. Your curse appears to be potent, and effective at keeping you alive."

I nodded.

"Kali doesn't do half-measures," I said. "The runic poisoning is being checked by the curse—for now."

"I think the transference of information would help you with that," she said. "Once we prepare your focus, you would be able to apply some of the knowledge to yourself and your poisoned condition."

"Kali said something similar to me a while back, about embracing who I am."

"She must have seen something in you to curse you this way."

"It's not exactly a reward," I said, thinking back to my recent conversation with Durga. "I interrupted a plan she had in the works for five thousand years."

"And she left you alive?"

"Somewhere in-between, it seems," I said, looking at Monty. "I don't know about this focus method, but we're going to have to deal with this poisoning at some point."

"We will," Monty said. "Once Fel is neutralized—"

"No, not *neutralized*," Orethe said, cutting him off. "Destroyed. Fel *must* be destroyed. Or your entire plane is at risk."

"We're not murderers," I said. "Isn't there—?"

"No. Weren't you paying attention?" she said with an edge to her voice. "*You* may not be murderers, but I can assure you, he is. He will exploit any weakness you expose. He will make you regret every breath you've allowed him, knowing you could have ended his existence and saved countless lives."

"Is that the voice of experience?" I asked. "You sound like you've run across him."

"Do you know why I'm in Elysium?"

"Something about gratuitous use of corpses to fulfill nefarious plans?"

"I was raising an army," she said, looking off to one side. "We had encountered Fel, a fully powered Revenant about to blast a sect, the Crimson Phoenix, a blood sect, out of existence. He had killed most of the lower level mages and was working his way up the sect's hierarchy."

"Blood mages?" I asked. "Do you mean sorcerers?"

"No, the Crimson Phoenix was the sect of mages that created the elder blood runes," she said. "They were powerful and dangerous. The runes were the reason they were targeted."

"You mean the lost runes?"

"They weren't lost then."

"Fel wanted the runes?"

"He wanted power," she said. "The blood runes would've made him unstoppable. Blood magic is volatile and powerful. It was why they were broken and then dispersed."

"Monty found one," I said, glancing his way. "How did that happen?"

"He found part of the rune of sealing, an incomplete rune."

"I thought it was incomplete," Monty said. "It felt like something was missing."

"Can you trace what you found?" she asked. "It should be safe here."

Monty traced the symbol.

She nodded.

"That is only part of the rune of sealing; it's missing a third section. The catalyst."

"York must have filled in that section with the Stormblood ritual," Monty said. "That must have been the catalyst."

"Along with his curse," she said, pointing at me. "Both aspects, the Stormblood and the curse, were powerful enough to act as a catalyst."

"And tethered Fel to us," Monty said. "How?"

"I don't know, yet," she said. "What I do know, is that the tether is a result of the blood rune, the Stormblood and the curse. Somehow I think it's the other way around. That ritual didn't tether Fel to you, it tethered you two to Fel."

"Nothing like being tethered to an insane power-hungry Revenant to brighten your day," I said. "Why haven't I ever heard of the Crimson Phoenix? Did Fel get to them all?"

"What remained of the sect was folded into the White Phoenix," Monty said. "From what I understand, it was only a handful of elders who survived the attack."

"Fel killed the rest?"

"Yes. Imagine hundreds, thousands, of dead bloodmages under his control. They would possess the full use of their fearsome abilities, but be mindless slaves to his whims, before he absorbed their life force."

"That would be a complete nightmare."

"And more," she said. "So I became proactive. When I arrived at the scene of the massacre, I turned the dead mages into an army under my control before he could. Fel went insane with fury, claiming I had robbed him of his rightful position."

"Did you?" I asked. "Was he some kind of heir?"

"All he was, was some kind of lunatic who thought he deserved more and more power," she said, looking at me. "I had nearly five hundred mages under my control."

"Was it enough?"

"Barely. We distracted him long enough for the elder blood rune of sealing to be used by the sect's elder mages, locking him behind the seal."

"How did that end you up here?" I said. "Sounds like you helped stop him."

She remained silent.

"The remaining elders voted for banishment?" Monty asked. "Or worse—"

"Execution," she finished. "After I risked my life, they wanted me dead. They concluded I was too much of a risk. Too dangerous to leave alive. Necromancers aren't exactly popular or well-liked. No matter that I had just saved their lives."

"What happened?"

"Once I heard the verdict, as you can imagine, I became somewhat upset," she said. "They were foolishly short-sighted, passing an edict while I still had control of the dead mages. They attempted to capture me; I disagreed violently."

"You killed them?"

"Not *all* of them," she said. "Just the elders who had voted for my termination. That was an oversight."

"And a capital offense for a mage," Monty added quietly. "Even more so for a necromancer."

"Like I gave a shit," Orethe snapped. "They wanted me dead. I was merely extending them the same courtesy."

"How did they stop you?" I asked. "You were controlling five hundred mages."

"The Ten intervened—specifically, Josephine," Orethe said. "She unleashed a Stormblood, disrupted my control for a few seconds. The rest of the Ten managed to incapacitate me further and detain me."

"How did she do that?" I asked. "That sounds impossible."

"For anyone else, perhaps. Not for her. Her Stormblood disintegrated all five hundred mages where they stood. The sudden severing of my link with them stunned me. It was enough to stop me."

"She killed five hundred mages?"

"No," Orethe said. "They were already dead. She merely finished the process and severed my control of them."

"Holy hell," I said under my breath. "I knew the Stormblood was strong, but I didn't know it was—"

"That is the power you two wield now," Orethe said. "I hope you never have to use it, but facing Fel? Nothing is off the table. *Nothing.*"

"We don't know how to use it yet," Monty said. "We are barely understanding the bond we now share."

"I suggest you accelerate the learning process," she said. "Fel is not going to wait patiently while you study the Stormblood."

"How did you avoid getting killed after that?"

"Exile," she said. "I was offered a choice. Exile here or death where I stood. I had been weakened and disoriented. There were still several elders alive and I was outnumbered. I chose exile."

"And they accepted your choice? Just like that?"

"The Ten can be a persuasive influence when they want to be," she said. "TK and LD spoke to Hades, brokered a deal, and this is now home."

"Do you miss it, your old plane?"

"No," she said. "We are doing this because of the threat Fel poses. After that, your training will commence."

"But I can't train here," I said. "This place inhibits your power."

"But it doesn't inhibit yours," she said with a wicked smile. "Your blast was powerful enough to punch a hole through me if I hadn't redirected it back at you. That is enough power to begin your training."

Hades appeared in the room.

"You have a situation that requires your immediate attention," he said. "Fel Sephtis is on the move."

SEVENTEEN

"What does that mean?" I asked. "On the move where, exactly?"

"Your city."

The icy grip of fear curled its fingers around my throat. For a few seconds, I found it hard to breathe.

"He's in the city?"

"He'll be targeting those closest to you," Hades said, his voice grim. "Using your link, he can find those places you frequent the most."

"How cut off is he, exactly? How much power does he have access to?"

"Right now, not much," Hades answered. "New York City is not very old and any major ley-lines would be buried too deep for him to access. He will try to accumulate power first."

"How? How does he do that?"

"The dead," Orethe said. "He'll target the dead. The more recent the better. He will use them to siphon energy and grow stronger."

"That's...that's just wrong."

"That's a Revenant," she said. "Especially Fel. He has no moral compass and if he ever did, he shattered it long ago."

"So this means—?"

"It means that, rather than bringing the fight to you," Hades said, "as he did at Scola Tower, he's trying to bring you to the fight."

"It's a lure," I said. "He can't attack us down here."

"He can't, and there's not much time left for me to explain," Hades said. "I can't be involved directly, but I will offer you all the assistance I can."

"A Revenant-ending spell would be useful right now."

"Apologies," Hades said with a small nod. "I don't have one of those, nor does anyone else."

"What about TK and LD?" I asked, looking around. "Are they coming?"

"No," Hades said. "Rest assured, they will be monitoring the situation, but you three will have the bulk of the work in stopping Fel."

"Basically, what you're saying is that we have to face Fel Sephtis on our own?"

"No, but you three will be the point of the spear," he said. "The others will be providing support and attacking other areas as well as providing area denial."

"That means, basically, we'll be facing Fel alone," I said. "At least until some kind of support shows up."

"For the most part, yes," he said. "Consider this advanced training."

"Advanced training is beginning to feel more and more like a suicide mission," I said. "Do we even have a chance against him?"

"If I didn't believe you had a chance, I wouldn't be sending you back," he answered. "Peaches will join you three in transit."

"In transit? What are you talking about in—"

We shifted from Orethe's guest bedroom in a blur of power. When the world stopped racing past us, we stood outside the Randy Rump.

A blown-up Randy Rump.

"That's some major teleporting," I said, as Monty shoved me to one side. "What the…?"

I landed on the street and rolled, as Monty formed violet orbs and blasted through two Shamblers who had mistaken me for lunch. A moment later, Peaches barreled into me, unleashing his baleful glare, cutting three more Shamblers down. They burst to dust as I rolled to my feet, drawing Grim Whisper.

<Thanks, boy.>

<You are my bondmate. I will keep you safe.>

<Make sure not to get near those things. I don't want them to hurt you.>

<The nice lady who smells like home made me many sausages. I am ready to fight.>

<Glad to hear it. Still, keep back. Use your omega beams or your bark. Don't let them touch you.>

<If I speak, it will hurt your ears.>

<Point it at them if there are too many. If not, use your beams.>

He sidled up to me and gave me a gentle nudge as I took stock of the situation.

The streets were uncharacteristically empty.

<This doesn't look good. Where are all the people?>

<The bad man is making them scared. The people don't want to come here.>

We stood on Ninth Avenue, the sun was setting, and the Randy Rump blazed with violet and black flames. My first thought was that Jimmy was going to be beyond pissed at the destruction.

Then I looked around and saw that the Rump was empty.

"He's in the backroom," Monty said. "The runes there proved too much for these Shamblers."

I breathed out a sigh of relief.

"Is it me, or is it odd that the streets are this empty?"

"It's not you," Orethe said, extending a hand and dropping a handful of Shamblers. "This is Fel's doing. His presence exudes an aura of death which keeps people away. He can't use his full abilities, but he still has access to some of his power."

"How much?" I asked. "How much access?"

"That much," she said and pointed up Ninth Avenue.

A small group of Shamblers had been forming.

I counted twenty, but more were materializing. Behind the Shamblers, I saw a nimbus of violet and black energy. In the center of the nimbus, I saw a figure, but couldn't make out the details.

"He's forming more Shamblers before he joins us himself," she said, pointing at the nimbus. "We need to interrupt that process."

I noticed a stream of violet energy flowing into the nimbus from above. I followed the stream with my gaze and saw it disappear over some buildings to my right.

"That's too much access," I said. "How is he doing that?"

"Is there a burial site nearby?" Orethe asked, looking around. "Dead bodies?"

"A burial site?"

"A cemetery. A place where bodies are buried?" she said, agitated, looking around us. "Is there one nearby? He's using the dead to fuel the siphon."

"No," I said—but then I remembered a small one close by. "Yes, on 11th, a few blocks away, but it's tiny."

"Doesn't matter, lead me there," she said. "We need to cut him off."

We ran east on 14th Street for several avenues, making a

left onto 6th Avenue until we hit 11th Street and a wall of black and violet energy.

The barrier cut off the street on both ends.

In the center of the street, in front of the Second Cemetery of Congregation Shearith Israel stood an Abomination with its arms outstretched to the sky.

Violet energy flowed out of the cemetery into the Abomination and then upward. I followed the trail of energy and saw another Abomination on a roof, also with its arms outstretched upward. The violet energy flowed into its body and out of its hands, arcing over the nearby buildings and out of sight.

"They're forming a chain," I said. "That's how Fel is accessing the power."

"This is the siphon, but it's weak."

"His power is increasing—incrementally, but it is increasing," Monty said, looking at the Abomination. "We need to interrupt that chain or he will continue draining this grave site."

"Yes," she said. "If he breaks the tether linking you, he won't need the Abominations, and no one in this city will be safe. Thankfully, this is an old and small cemetery."

"Why is age a factor?"

"It's too old to provide enough energy to get him to full power."

"One of the oldest," I said. "He must have targeted this one because it's the closest one to the Rump. What happens if he finds a larger cemetery?"

"We can't allow him near any large gathering of the dead," she said, her voice ominous. "Especially the recently deceased. That would be catastrophic."

"There aren't that many cemeteries in the city," I said. "As far as I know, none of them allow people to be buried in them. We should be able to head him off before he grows in power."

"I'm not just referring to graves," she said, looking around. "Where is the morgue? A city this size must have several large ones. Is there one close by?"

"The New York City Mortuary is between 26th and 28th off First Avenue," I said, staring uptown. "Shit, that's close to—"

"Haven," Monty said, his expression dark. "Do I even want to know why you know the location of morgues and cemeteries? That's not exactly common knowledge."

"No, you don't, not really," I said, before turning to Orethe. "Are the morgues a target?"

"They are sources of energy for him, or any necromancer like him," she said. "That's where he'll be headed next as he grows in power."

"That sounds bad. Tell me why that sounds bad."

"Did you see Dawn of the Dead?"

"Romero or the remake?"

"The remake," she said. "The ones with the undead that learned to run at top speed."

"No," I said as a cold dread filled me. "Is that what we're looking at?"

"Yes," she said. "The Shamblers evolve as Fel increases his power. They won't be shambling, and after he reaches a certain level of power; they will begin to replicate and drain the living. In a matter of weeks, maybe a few months, this city will belong to Fel."

"The morgue at Haven is no ordinary morgue," Monty said. "Some of the bodies there belong to supernatural creatures."

"That will make it worse," Orethe said. "If he can perform a binding ritual, he will be able to reform them into a twisted, mutated form of their abilities as well."

"Fel is like the sickness that just keeps giving," I said. "This is bad."

"They're like a virus," Monty said. "Replicating and draining life, powering Fel and duplicating themselves."

"I've seen that," I said, looking through the barrier. "How do we get past this? How do we stop it?"

"Destroy Fel and the entire process ends," she said. "He is the key."

"We're not going to destroy anything unless we can get past this wall," I said, examining the barrier in front of us. "Monty, you think you can get through—?"

Orethe raised a finger.

"Give me a few moments," she said. "I can get through this wall. Get ready. Once it's down, we'll be under attack."

She knelt down in front of the barrier and began tracing symbols on the floor next to it while saying something under her breath.

"She doesn't finger-wiggle?" I asked as she worked. I looked around, but the streets were eerily empty. It was a bad sign. "I thought for sure she would—"

"She's a necromancer, not a mage," Monty said, peering past the barrier at the flow of energy and the Abomination absorbing it. "She uses runes like a mage, but also has a focus somewhere on her person, allowing her to channel her power."

"I didn't see a staff or anything like that," I said, looking at Orethe. "Maybe it's hidden?"

"A focus is any item she has imbued to act as the locus of her power, amplifying it."

"So it can literally be any—?"

My phone rang as the Abomination behind the barrier turned its head to focus on me. I pulled out my phone and connected the call without looking at the number.

That was a mistake.

"Whoever this is, kind of busy at the moment," I continued before I heard the voice. "Call you right—"

"Don't you dare," Ramirez's growl came over the line. "I have just had reports of zombies on the streets of my city, Strong. Explain this to me, now."

"Zombies?" I said lightheartedly. "You've been watching too many movies, Angel. Zombies don't exist."

Orethe shot me a glance that said: *Are you serious right now? Get off the phone. We're in the middle of trying not to die.*

"You're lying," Ramirez said. "Know how I know? One of my men got too close to one of your imaginary zombies, and you know what happened?"

"I have an idea, yes. How close did he get?"

"Drop-dead close," Ramirez said, his voice serious. Angel hated many things, most of them supernatural, but what he hated the most was losing his people. "Don't bullshit me, Strong. What are these things?"

"They're not zombies," I said, dropping the act and matching his tone. "They *are* dangerous. Keep your people away from them. If you have to confront, keep it long distance. Whatever you do, do not engage in close quarters."

"Thank you, Captain Obvious. Tell me something I don't know," he said over the din of activity. "How do we stop them?"

"Working on it," I said, and regretted it instantly. "I mean, I'm just as surprised as you."

"So you *are* part of this," he said. "What did you *do*?"

"What did I do? Nothing," I said. "Look, Angel, keep your people away from these things and I will keep you in the loop of what I'm doing and what I'm learning, I promise."

"So you want me to sit here and twiddle my fingers until you figure it out?" he said with a growl. "You need to give me more than that. I have people dying out here. I'm not going to sit here and watch them turn to dust."

"No, you can cordon off all the cemeteries and morgues in the city and the surrounding areas around each for at least four to five blocks around each. Start with Haven."

"I don't have that kind of manpower."

"Coordinate and get it," I said. "Because if you don't, this is going to get worse. Much worse."

"How bad is it, Strong?" he asked. "Give it to me straight."

There was no way I was ever going to give it to him straight about anything we encountered, but he was my friend and I wanted him to be safe.

Even if he didn't listen.

For once, I was going to be honest with him—or at least, more honest.

"If Haven falls, we need to start thinking about evacuating the city."

"Strong, this is no time for jokes," he said with a nervous laugh. "You're joking, right? There's no way we can evacuate this city."

"Then we all die," I said. "Some will die right away and some later, but that will be the outcome. That straight enough for you?"

"Understood," he said after a pause. "I'll send several teams to Haven with instructions to lock it down."

"These creatures will kill anyone they come in contact with...anyone. Body armor won't work. Really, the only thing you and the NYTF should do is keep back, and make sure no one else gets close."

I hoped it was enough of a warning, but knowing Ramirez, he would just figure out a way to lob grenades at the Shamblers from a distance.

"We'll keep back until we can find a safe way to blow these things apart," he said. "Until then we'll close off the cemeteries and morgues as best we can, starting with Haven."

"Thank you," I said. "I mean it, Angel. Stay away from these things."

"We will," he said. "You can thank me by stopping whatever nightmare this is. My team is going to need therapy for months after this. I already have a few who cracked after Jenkins rushed in and got himself dusted."

"Sorry to hear that. Keep the fragile ones away. Everyone else needs to avoid CQC wherever possible," I said as I noticed another Abomination join the first one. "Gotta go."

"Strong, don't get dead."

"I'll do my best," I said, ending the call. "NYTF is on its way to lock down Haven. What the hell is that?"

"It seems like a new and improved version of what we faced at Scola Tower," Monty said. "I take it the NYTF has encountered Shamblers?"

"Yes, though I don't think they've seen these handsome monsters yet," I said. "Angel lost someone to a Shambler. He got too close and was drained."

"Roxanne will lockdown Haven, but I'd best make sure."

I dialed Roxanne's direct number and put it on speakerphone.

"Simon, do you have something to do with the creatures I keep hearing about?" Roxanne said after the call connected. "They appear to be reanimations."

"They are," Monty said. "Have you initiated a lockdown?"

"I've always disliked necromancy. It's the dealing with the recently revived dead. I find it—"

"Gross?" I offered. "Glad I'm not the only one."

"I was going to say distasteful."

"Same thing."

"The lockdown," Monty said, giving me a look. "Is it in place?"

"Several hours ago, as is standard protocol," she said. "I'm needed downstairs. It's good to hear your voice. Whatever this is, make sure you stop it."

"On the top of my list," he said, and then paused. "Be careful."

"I'm not the one facing whatever these things are. Please keep safe."

Monty ended the call and handed me the phone as he stared past the barrier.

The second Abomination was larger than the one we'd faced at Scola Tower. It was just as hideous, covered in black energy, but appeared even more dangerous as arcs of electricity crisscrossed its body. The pungent smell of chlorine filled the air, which I assumed was an effect of the power coursing through its body.

"The electricity is new," I said. "Upgrade?"

"Indeed," Monty said, narrowing his eyes at the creature. "I'd say the electrical component of this entity bears avoiding."

"Right, don't get hit by the lightning," I said. "Good thing you told me."

"Montague, Strong, and *Orethe?*" the second Abomination said, focusing on her. "Is that you? It truly has been too long. I'm surprised you're still alive—a condition I will rectify once I'm restored. I haven't forgotten your interference when I faced the Crimson Phoenix."

Fel Sephtis.

"Massacred," Orethe said. "You massacred them."

"Semantics," the Fel-Abomination said, approaching the barrier as the blue arcs of power crackled all over its body. "They were in my way and needed to be removed."

"So you annihilated them," Orethe said as she continued working. "So kind of you."

"As I recall," he said, "*you* were the cause of their ultimate demise. You stole them from me."

"After *you* killed them," she said. "Let's not forget that small point."

"You wanted the power of the elder runes as much as I did. Let's not lie to ourselves."

"No," Orethe said, looking up for a moment at the Abomination controlled by Fel. "I never wanted the power. All I wanted was to be left alone. You hungered for the power; it was never enough for you."

"Yet, here you are," he said, turning to Monty and me. "Do they know what you did with the lost elder rune of sealing?"

"I did what I needed to do," she said, returning her focus to the barrier. "What was necessary."

"They *don't* know," he said, still looking at Monty and me. "You didn't share, and you say you aren't here for the power. Would you like me to tell them?"

"It doesn't matter," she said. "I'm here to end you, once and for all."

"That remains to be seen," he said, stepping back next to the other Abomination. "You don't have five hundred mages at your disposal this time."

"I don't need five hundred mages for you," she said, her voice full of menace. "You're only alive because the Ten interfered last time. This time…this time it ends."

"Empty threats," he said. "You've been in your gilded cage for too long. You can't face me. Even in my current, diminished state, I'm too much for you—much less some upstart child of a mage, the clueless pawn of a goddess, and some infernal runt. This is an insult."

"I'd love nothing more than to face you, Fel," she said. "Why are you hiding behind barriers and puppets?"

"We'll meet soon enough. You will beg me to end your existence quickly, but I won't. I'll make sure to take my time," he said with a snarl. "You will all belong to me. Everyone in this wretched city will fall before me."

"Still using the same old threats?" She stood and took a few steps back. "Boring, Fel. You sound like a spoiled child lamenting the loss of his favorite toys. You're pathetic."

The Abomination roared. Larger arcs of power mixed with black energy jumped off its body, scorching the concrete and asphalt.

"Was that smart?" I asked. "Pissing him off like that?"

"Smart?" she said with a wicked smile. "Smart would have been staying home, away from all this mess. No, being here is not smart in the least. However, most of those who allow themselves to be controlled by power have such fragile egos, that it's hard to resist."

"Can we take him?" I asked, keeping my eyes focused on the seething Fel-Abomination. "That electricity looks dangerous."

"We? No," she said, cracking her neck and shaking out her hands. "This one is mine."

EIGHTEEN

"You can't be serious," Monty said. "Facing that creature alone is unwise."

"I'm not alone," she said. "I have you two"—she glanced down at Peaches—"three, here with me."

"I don't think you going up against—" I started before she waved my words away.

"This barrier is going to come down in the next ten seconds," Orethe said under her breath. "When it does, you and your hound focus on the first Abomination, not the one being controlled by Fel."

"What are you going to do?" I asked. "The other one is covered in black energy and electrical power."

"I'm aware," she said. "Mage Montague and I will go after Fel's puppet. We divide and conquer."

"Or get blasted to bits," I said. "Good chance of that."

"No risk, no reward," she said, flexing her fingers. "Get ready. The energy is about to surge and bring the barrier down."

"What did he mean about you and the elder rune of sealing?" Monty asked. "What did you do with it?"

"No time to explain," she said, standing and stepping back. "If we survive this, I'll show you everything. Right now, we have larger worries."

The barrier continued to fall.

"Remember, we have to disrupt this siphon, or we're just wasting our time," she said. "Strong, break that flow of energy. I'll deal with Fel's puppet. Montague, follow my lead and we'll finish this."

Monty gave her a short nod and adjusted his sleeves.

At least she sounded confident.

I was beginning to understand that rushing into imminent death wasn't just a mage thing. It seemed like everyone who wielded power had an intense deathwish.

It wasn't lost on me that I was doing plenty of rushing toward pain and death instead of the smart thing, which would've been rushing *away* from a creature that could probably rip my arms off and beat me silly with them.

I shook my head, drew Grim Whisper and glanced down at my hellhound.

<*You ready?*>

Peaches growled next to me as the barrier fell.

<*Can I bite this one?*>

<*This one you can bite. Don't let it hit you.*>

<*I won't. It smells bad.*>

<*I'm sure it does. Be careful.*>

We rushed forward as the barrier fell. Peaches blinked out next to me and reappeared, smashing into the chest of the first Abomination. He bounced off with no effect. I opened fire as I advanced.

I may as well have been firing cotton balls for all the effect my rounds had. I didn't even get the Abomination's attention. I holstered Grim Whisper and focused, drawing on my power.

Peaches growled again, this time louder, creating tremors

around us. The Abomination siphoning the energy from the cemetery looked at him. Peaches hunched his shoulders and crouched down as the runes along his flanks glowed a dim red. His paws sank into the asphalt of the street before he launched himself forward.

I raised a hand and waited.

I needed to time it perfectly. Once Peaches crashed into the siphoning Abomination, I would hit it with a magic missile, for a one-two-punch attack.

I gathered energy and waited.

The Abomination lowered one arm as Peaches closed. Peaches leapt in the air and the Abomination swung his arm as I yelled, "*Ignis vitae!*"

Several things happened after that.

The Abomination timed the arc of Peaches' jump and unleashed an uppercut that connected, sending him out of sight over the nearest building.

My magic missile blasted out of my hand, throwing me off balance with more force than I expected, drilling into the Abomination, and blowing a chunk of his chest away from his body.

In a rage, I formed Ebonsoul and closed on the Abomination, screaming, furious that I told Peaches to get close enough to bite this monster.

As I closed the distance, I heard my name being called.

Peaches reappeared, blinking in next to me and shoving me to one side with his massive head. An arc of black energy interlaced with electricity crackled into my side, spinning and slamming me into the wall of the cemetery with enough force to crack several of the large stones.

If Peaches hadn't shoved me to one side, I would've caught the full force of the blast. I looked down at my bloody side. A gaping hole was surrounded by burnt flesh. My body flushed into an inferno as I slid down the wall, and my vision becoming blurry as I reabsorbed Ebonsoul.

"Shit, that...that hurt."

The world tilted sideways.

Peaches unleashed his omega beams and blasted what was left of the siphoning Abomination. The creature crumpled to the ground as the Fel-Abomination roared into the night.

I ended up in a seated position and fell to my side. My head gently tapped the ground a few times. A few moments passed, before I was assaulted again with hellhound slobber.

<*My saliva will heal you.*>

<*I'll be fine. I just...I just need some time. Are you okay? That Abomination launched you over a building. I thought I lost you.*>

<*I ate many sausages. I am very strong. You can never lose me. I am your bondmate.*>

I was feeling better by the second as my body repaired itself, but I felt weak. We had managed our part, the siphon was interrupted. I sat up and managed unsteadily to get to my feet. The world swayed again, forcing me to use the wall for support until the street decided to level out.

<*Go help Monty and Orethe. That Abomination is stronger.*>

<*I have to keep you safe.*>

<*I'm safe. Go help them, or we're all in trouble.*>

He blinked out a second later.

He reappeared next to Orethe and fired an omega beam at the remaining Abomination. The beam hit the larger creature full force and bounced off its skin.

This wasn't going to be easy.

That's when I heard the screeching. It filled the night like nails on an enormous chalkboard.

The sound was getting closer.

"Monty," I called out, "we have incoming."

"A little busy at the moment," he replied as he dodged a blast of arc energy and launched a barrage of white orbs at the Abomination to no effect. He turned to Orethe. "We need to retreat. It's too strong."

Orethe shook her head.

"It's reinforced because Fel is controlling it," she said, placing a hand on her chest. "Create an opening and I'll do the rest."

No matter what Monty threw at it, the Abomination managed to deflect, dodge, or withstand. Peaches' omega beams were more of a nuisance to it than anything else.

I considered unleashing another magic missile for close to half a second before I realized that would be a bad idea. Because of the damage I had suffered, I had just about enough energy to launch another one before I passed out.

That left Ebonsoul.

There was no way I wanted to stab the Fel-Abomination. Aside from the fact that getting close enough to cut it meant getting within face-smashing distance, I had no desire to siphon whatever energy was powering that thing. It felt bad enough from where I stood. I didn't want anymore of it inside me.

I was going to have to get creative.

I materialized Ebonsoul, forming a silver mist around my arm.

I had an idea.

I focused and gathered the energy to form another magic missile, my body screaming in protest as I did so. Leaving Ebonsoul as a mist around my hand, I aimed and whispered, "*Ignis vitae.*"

The draw of energy on my body was more than I could handle. I fell to one knee, my breathing ragged, as my vision tunneled in. I kept my arm extended and focused on the Fel-Abomination.

A beam of black, violet, and silver energy exploded from my hand, heading for the Abomination. The creature turned in my direction, sensing the energy expenditure, and prepared another lightning blast to finish barbecuing me.

My enhanced Ebonsoul missile cut through the Abomination's side, removing an arm and causing it to roar in agony.

"Payback's a bitch," I said, falling forward. It was a good thing the concrete was there to break my fall. "Your turn, Orethe."

She was already moving.

A bright violet-and-yellow glow erupted from the area she touched on her chest. She raced close to the Abomination and placed a palm along its chest.

The light she created enveloped the Abomination and began dissolving it. The energy she released devoured the Abomination in under ten seconds. More roars filled the night as the Shamblers answered with an ear-splitting screech.

I felt Monty lift me to my feet.

"Remind me not to piss her off," I said, slurring some words and looking at the pile of dust that used to be the Abomination. "She's dangerous."

"This entire neighborhood has suddenly become quite dangerous," he said, wrapping an arm under my armpit and over my shoulder. "Orethe?"

"Right behind you," she called out. "Go!"

Monty formed a circle under us.

Peaches bounded into the circle as the world shifted in a haze of green.

NINETEEN

We appeared in front of the Randy Rump.

The flames had long since gone, but the damage was extensive. I would have preferred a teleport somewhere else.

"You couldn't have ported us somewhere more beachy?" I asked as Monty kept me on my feet. "You know, somewhere tropical, without psychotic Revenants trying to kill us?"

"Maybe some other time," he said, examining the exterior of the Rump. "They tried to breach the defenses. That was a mistake."

"Looks like they did some serious damage," I said, feeling better as my curse worked overtime. "They couldn't get in."

"Nothing that can't be repaired," he said. "The rune work did an exceptional job of keeping the place mostly intact."

"I'm pretty sure this will get pinned on us," I said, surveying the damage. "Doesn't matter, that we had nothing to do with it this time."

"We're convenient scapegoats," Monty said, disabling the defensive runes that protected the back room. "It appears to be mostly cosmetic. The runes dealt with most of the flames."

"What did you do?" Orethe said, stepping up to me. "How did you damage the second Abomination?"

I took a step back.

"Whoa, slow down," I said, raising a hand. "I used my blade, Ebonsoul."

"I saw no blade," she said, looking into my eyes. "There was no weapon at all."

"You're the one who melted the Abomination," I said. "What was that yellow light?"

"My focus," she said, touching the right side of her chest. It gave off a soft yellow-and-violet glow. "I had a bloodgem focus imbued with power and embedded under my skin. Fel has one as well. Can you show me your weapon?"

I extended my arm and let the silver mist of Ebonsoul gather around my hand. A moment later, it materialized.

"You blended this blade with the magic missile, using it to enhance the blast," she said, looking at my arm. "It seems to have activated the poison in your system."

The dark lines in my arms were darker and deeper, the violet shining a little brighter. None of that made me feel comfortable.

"I know," I said, looking at my arms. "It was a lucky guess. You needed an opening. I tried to make one."

"And then some," Monty said, glancing at the dark lines in my arm. "We'll have to look into that in depth. This poison is resisting your curse."

"Sure, right after we aren't fighting energy-draining zombies trying to siphon our lives to feed the psycho Revenant. We can conduct tests and everything."

"The first chance we get," Monty said, still looking at my arms, "you're going to be admitted into Haven for observation."

"Not a big fan of that idea," I said. "Haven's track record with attacks sucks. How about we contact Quan?"

Monty nodded.

"A reasonable assessment and solution."

"You are full of surprises, Simon Strong," Orethe said.

"So are you," I said, reabsorbing Ebonsoul. "How do you know Fel has a bloodgem focus like yours?"

"Similar, but different," she said. "Our schools of necromancy share a common root. Pure necromancers use bloodgems to focus our power. Reanimators—what Fel is—use them to store their power."

"If we remove his bloodgem, would it stop him?"

"No," she said, shaking her head. "It would weaken him for a time, but he could create another. I told you, stopping him is not an option. We have to kill him."

Another thought crossed my mind.

"What happens if *you* lose your bloodgem?"

"For pure necromancers, like me, losing a bloodgem means losing control of our abilities, our focus. The power I possess would overcome me, ending my life. It would be a painful death."

"We need to make sure that doesn't happen, then," I said, my voice low. "Do you know where his bloodgem is?"

She placed her hand on the opposite side of her chest.

"Over his heart," she said. "They make direct use of blood. It's why he attacked the Crimson Phoenix in the first place, and why he wanted their runes."

"Great, all we need to do is remove his bloodgem and maybe his heart," I said. "That should make him weak enough to end this insanity."

"Not necessarily," Monty said. "Necromancers are infamous for avoiding death. It's part of who and what they are. They are notoriously difficult to kill."

Orethe nodded and looked up.

"He'll head to the morgue next," Orethe said, her voice grim as Monty headed to the back room to the Randy Rump.

"Fel's been delayed, but we can't stay here long. He'll regroup and if he gets access to a morgue—"

"I need to make sure Jimmy and his people are okay," I said, following Monty. "Give me ten minutes. We can spare ten minutes."

"Ten minutes, no more," she said. "He'll be disoriented for a short time. Once he recovers we need to be at this morgue, or Haven, wherever it is."

"We can get there from here in about ten minutes," I said.

She nodded and examined the destruction of the Rump.

Monty manipulated the runes on the enormous door, deactivating the defenses and unlocking the door. He pulled it open and we both stepped back in reaction to the energy signature that filled the Rump.

Peaches growled by my side.

Jimmy stepped out of the back room.

He was not happy.

I realized this first because of my amazing deductive abilities. Also, the fact that I was looking up at an enormous grizzly bear made for another definite clue.

Monty immediately formed several violet orbs. Orethe put her hand to her chest, causing the area to turn yellow again. I let my hand rest on Grim Whisper, but kept it holstered.

The bear came roaring out of the back room and came up short when he saw it was us, skidding to a stop a few feet away.

Everything I knew about shifters, which wasn't much, told me that they didn't always become mindless once shifted. I may have been looking at the largest grizzly I had ever seen, but under all that fur, and behind those razor-sharp claws, it was still Jimmy the Butcher.

He shifted back almost immediately, his clothes reforming as he assumed human form. It seemed to be a powerful component of his shifting, judging from the increased energy signature, as he reverted back to a towering, angry man in overalls.

"I almost killed you," he said in a semi-growl. "What are you doing here and where are those zombies?"

"Shamblers," I said. "You and your people need to evacuate the premises, now. They're coming back soon."

Jimmy shook his head.

"No safer place around here than that backroom," he said, thumbing over his shoulder. "We have everything we need. Food, facilities, and defense. Nothing short of a runic nuclear attack is going to get through those defenses."

I glanced at Monty.

"He has a point," Monty confirmed. "Once the defenses are active, that back room is nearly impregnable. It would take an Archmage several hours to get through them, if at all. Shamblers and Abominations would have no chance, even enhanced ones."

"How long can you hunker down in there?" I asked, turning back to Jimmy. "How long can you last in there without opening the door?"

"We have enough supplies to last us about a month," he said, looking into the room. "Grohn is away visiting his people. It's just me and two others, Artis and Dov. You think this whole thing is going to last longer than that?"

"I really hope not," I said as two figures emerged from the back room. "If it does, then we have officially entered a nightmare scenario. Artis and Dov?"

Jimmy nodded.

"Artis," he said, pointing to the male, "and his sister, Dov."

It was easy to see they were siblings. Both were tall and muscular, the female slightly less muscular than the male. Both had long brown hair and piercing green eyes, and both wore Randy Rump uniforms as they approached.

Their energy signatures were similar to Jimmy's. I assumed they were shifters as well. They both wore nervous expressions and looked apprehensive. It felt like they were one Shambler screech away from shifting into bears and attempting to shred us.

Jimmy looked back at them and waved them down.

"These are friendlies," Jimmy said. "This here is Simon Strong"—he motioned to me—"and Mage Tristan Montague."

"Are you a real mage?" Dov asked Monty. "You can perform magic?"

Monty nodded.

"You'll have to excuse them," Jimmy apologized. "They don't get out much."

"That's no regular dog," Artis said, staring and pointing at Peaches. "He smells powerful." He looked at me. "Is he yours?"

"Sometimes I think it's the other way around," I answered. "You're right, though—he's not a regular dog."

"The pup is a hellhound," Jimmy said. "His name is Peaches."

"A hellhound? Really?" Artis asked. "I hear they're extra rare. Did you say Peaches?"

"Yes," I said. "The name came with the hound, so I rolled with it."

"If you didn't name him, who did?"

I thought back to how happy Persephone was to see my hellhound and figured she had a hand in his naming…especially when I realized Hades had named his hellhound *Spot*. With that much creativity flowing around, Peaches would've ended up being named *Dog* or something equally profound, if it had been up to Hades.

"I'm going guess and say Persephone did," I answered. "It makes the most sense."

"You're saying a goddess named him?" Dov asked, clearly unconvinced. "Hades' wife? That Persephone?"

"Only one I know," I said. "Go ahead, you can pet him. If he doesn't like it, he'll let you know."

"Thank you," they both said and approached my hellhound.

The siblings immediately relaxed, even smiling as they flanked Peaches and rubbed his sides—which he allowed, being the ham that he was.

I stepped away and turned to Jimmy.

"They're—?" I started.

"From my original sleuth, yes," Jimmy confirmed. "Shifters like me. Can you explain what is going on?" He glanced over at Orethe. "Who is she?"

"We don't have that kind of time, sorry," I said. "I can give you the condensed version."

He nodded, still looking at Orethe.

"Do you know what a Revenant is?"

"I'm familiar, yes."

"A Revenant wants to kill me and Monty so he can be free to pretty much kill everything else."

"He can't be free until he kills you two?"

"We're bonded through a ritual too complicated for me to explain, but yes, he needs us dead before he can access all of his power."

He sniffed the air, his expression turning dark.

"She's going to help you?" he asked. "Do you know what she is?"

"Yes," I said, glancing at Orethe. "She's a heavy-hitting necromancer. Her name is Orethe, and she's going to help us stop him."

"You've joined a necromancer to fight another necromancer?" he asked. "Isn't that a little like asking an arsonist to help you put out fire?"

"I get that necromancers aren't liked."

"Hated and reviled is closer to it," he said, still glancing her way. "I'm not passing any judgment. Just wondering why you would join *with* her to fight an undead uprising."

"More like she joined us, but that's the general idea."

"Are you sure that's a good idea?" he asked. "Necromancers aren't known for being team players unless they are the ones creating the teams. Usually from dead enemies."

"Yes," I said, glancing at Orethe. "Seems to be the only way to do this. I'm not a necromancer and neither is Monty, and she hasn't given us a reason to distrust her."

"Yet," he said, shaking his head. "This sounds like a bad idea, Simon. I've had run-ins with necros in the past. Have yet to find one I could trust."

"You have an alternative?" I asked. "I understand that shifters have been killed in the past—"

"Hunted and killed," he said, his words filled with anger and pain. "For sport. Do you know how powerful an undead shifter can be?"

"I would imagine fairly powerful."

"You don't want to run into one—ever. Trust me."

"Not *every* necromancer is evil," I said. "There have to be a few good ones, even if the odds are against it. She seems like one of the good ones, or at the very least, she isn't going around trying to raise an undead army."

Except for that one time when she did try to raise an undead army.

"We'll see. Like I said, no judgment," he replied. "If you say she's going to help you deal with this threat, I'll take your word and count her as one of the few good ones...until proven otherwise."

"Thanks. That's all I ask."

"Is she strong enough to stop him?" Jimmy asked looking at Orethe. "We saw some pretty nasty creatures, but we didn't meet whatever or whoever was controlling them, that much I know."

"She's plenty strong," I said. "Plus, we're going to help her."

"Are you four going to be enough?" he asked. "Don't get me wrong, you three have earned your title—The Trio of Terror—but you seem outnumbered on this one. Why not call in the Dark Council or the NYTF?"

"Normally, I would agree."

"But?"

"The Dark Council is one-third vampire. Necromancers and undead?"

"You think he would take them over?" Jimmy asked. "Has that happened before?"

"I don't know, but confronting a necromancer with a large group of undead doesn't sound like the best idea," I answered. "Don't want to take that chance."

"You sure know how to make enemies," he said, taking one last look at Orethe before turning away. "And friends."

"It's a gift, or really I should say, it's a curse," I said. "Might be better to keep the vampires, mages, and werewolves out of this one. Especially vampires."

"Can you? You know they're going to hear about this sooner or later," he said, looking at the exterior of the Randy Rump. "It's going to be kind of hard to hide the damage if these Shamblers start spreading."

"We're here to stop that from happening. The Dark Council and me aren't exactly on speaking terms at the moment."

"They're still pissed at you?" he asked, then paused. "Is *she* still pissed at you?"

"Something like that," I said, nodding. "We haven't really smoothed out our last situation since Japan. Last I heard, she's in the city and restructuring the Dark Council along with some renovations downtown. I don't want to involve the Council until she and I speak, and besides, we have backup."

"Where?" Jimmy asked, looking around. "I only see you four. Where is the backup?"

"I'm sure they'll arrive when we need them the most," I assured him. "If not, well, this is going to be an extremely short mission."

"Simon," Orethe said. "We need to go."

I nodded and turned to Jimmy.

"If you're going to be okay in the back room, you need to get back in there and activate the defenses, now. We have more nastiness headed this way."

He extended his massive hand and I took it. We shook before he ushered Artis and Dov away from Peaches and into the back room. He gave me one last nod before entering and closing the door behind him.

I took note of the runes Monty pressed to reactivate the defenses. The runes gave off a golden light as he pressed them in sequence.

"They should be safe," Monty said. "These defenses are robust."

"What happens if someone or something tries to get in there again?" I asked. "What will the defenses do? I mean, the place is exploded."

"I modified the defenses somewhat," Monty said, looking at the rest of the interior of the Rump. "If the runes on this door are tampered with, the results would be explosive."

"Isn't that what happened the first time?" I asked, following his gaze around the Rump with my own. "They tried to get in and the runes exploded?"

"No," he said, looking at me. "The flames were a deterrent, a first line of defense, which is why this damage is mostly cosmetic. If the defenses on this door are tampered with now, we'd have to build Jimmy a new Randy Rump after the runes are set off."

"That bad?"

"Only the back room, and this door would survive the blast," he said. "Everything else would be rubble."

"Right. Let's try and avoid that then," I said. "Last thing we need is a mega-explosion *and* Shamblers coming after us."

"Agreed."

As if on cue, screeches filled the night.

TWENTY

"Why would Fel target the Rump?" I asked as we headed uptown. "It holds no specific relevance. It's not built over a cemetery or a place of power."

"It's obvious," Orethe said. "That place holds significance for you two. He will target those places you frequent. Remember, his objective is your elimination."

We moved at a quick run.

Well, I tried to move at a quick run. It turned out to be a slow jog as the pain in my side increased. The sweat poured into my eyes, accompanying the pain in my side. I glanced at the wound site and saw that the skin was still raw and red. The poison in my blood was still interfering with my healing.

"Tell me again why we're not using the Dark Goat, or, at the very least a teleport?" I asked, semi-wincing with every step. "Just curious, since this running isn't exactly helping me heal any faster."

"No time to get the vehicle. Also, I think it would be unwise to lead any Shamblers to the Moscow," Monty said. "Olga would be most displeased."

I shuddered at the thought of an angry Olga coming after us for leading Shamblers to her domain.

"Let's not piss off the ice-queen landlord today," I said. "We have enough things after us. What about a teleport?"

I couldn't believe I was actually requesting a teleport.

"As for teleporting, there is no way to gauge the extent of our connection to Fel. The expenditure of energy involved in a teleport may alert him to our exact location. Something we should avoid at all costs."

"I hate it when you make sense," I said with a growl. "Are we doing the mortuary or Haven? It's two separate locations."

"The mortuary, I think, "Monty said. "Haven will be locked down. Recent events have given Roxanne reason to increase security. No one is getting in there easily, even with an army of Shamblers and Abominations. The mortuary will be the easier target of the two."

"Which means Fel will head there first."

"I agree," Orethe said. "Fel will go for the easier target at his current level of strength, considering we interrupted the siphon."

"How long until he appears?" I asked, keeping my eyes open for any undead roaming the streets. They were still eerily empty. "I'm not talking about his Abominations—I mean Fel, in person."

"We don't want that to happen," Orethe said. "That would be...bad."

"With the power he siphoned from the cemetery, how much stronger is he now?" I asked as I felt a spike of energy behind me. "How close to max is he?"

I slowed down and turned to look behind us.

"He's nowhere near his maximum level," Orethe said. "If he were, we'd be facing an army of Abominations and Shamblers right now, with Fel leading them."

"Nothing like a hands-on leader," I said, pointing to

the mob a few blocks away. "That looks like a large number of Shamblers. Not an army, but nothing to sneeze at, either."

Monty turned and peered into the night.

"That is a sizable group of Shamblers; no Abominations as far as I can tell," he said. "Still, they pose a significant threat in large numbers."

We were standing on the corner of Third Avenue and 20th Street. Three blocks behind us, easily visible in the night, the large group of Shamblers were following us up Third.

They gave off a sickly, pale blue glow, and numbered about a hundred as they converged on us. As Monty pointed out, I didn't see any Abominations in the group, thankfully, but it didn't make me feel any better knowing we were being chased by the undead.

Are they chasing all of us?

Somehow, this whole situation of undead roaming the streets creeped me out.

"He must have siphoned more than I thought," Orethe said. "We need to keep moving."

I remained where I stood.

"I'm not comfortable leading them to the mortuary or Haven," I said, staring at the undead mob. "Who are they really after right now?"

"You," Orethe said without hesitation. "You currently present the greatest energy signature. Your life force is a beacon of power to them in this state. It would be like dangling a piece of meat before a hungry—"

"Hellhound?"

"Sure, that works," she said. "If they caught up to you, they would siphon you until you were a husk, all the while feeding Fel your life force. Since you're cursed alive, it would mean—"

"They could siphon enough power to restore Fel completely."

She nodded.

"They're still moving quite slowly," she said, looking at the Shamblers. He must have chosen numbers in order to overwhelm us."

"If they're that focused on me, that means I can lead them away while you two head to the mortuary and stop that binding ritual Fel needs to power up."

"That is a bad idea," Monty said, shaking his head. "If they overrun you, Fel will be restored to full power. We should stay to—"

"I have Peaches," I said, cutting him off. "If it gets dicey, he can blink me out of there."

"He's right," Orethe said. "He can buy us time to set up the counter-ritual before Fel tries to bind to the dead." She looked at me and then down at my wound. "Can you really avoid the Shamblers?"

I looked back at the mob of creatures heading our way. They were moving, but it was slow going. They weren't close to the speed of the Shamblers on Scola Tower, which meant Fel was still low on power.

As long as they kept this pace, I could stay ahead of them.

"I can lead them away," I said with a nod. "Without letting them catch up."

"Keep away from populated areas if you can," Orethe said. "They won't attack the living, yet, and I doubt any normals could even see them, but it's best to be on the safe side. Right now, all they want is you—well, actually, your life force."

"Are you saying they only want me for my body?"

"No, what I'm saying is—"

Monty placed a hand on her arm.

"Don't encourage him," he said, shaking his head. "It's not a real question."

"The burden of being popular," I said with a tight smile. "One more thing I need to thank Kali for, wonderful."

"Do not let them catch you," Monty said. "At the first sign of trouble, you and your creature reconvene on us."

"At the *first* sign?" I asked, glancing at the approaching Shamblers. "You mean the recent events don't indicate we have reached the first sign? I thought a horde of hungry zombies made a pretty good first sign."

"They are not zombies and this is not a movie," Orethe snapped. "Focus. If they get ahold of you, it's over."

"No worries. At the first or maybe the second sign of trouble, I'll head right over to you."

"You know what I meant," Monty said, his voice and expression serious. "Keep moving and try to lead them back downtown if you can. The further away from us, the better."

"Got it," I said with a nod. "Get going."

They took off at a faster run. I knew I had been slowing them down.

I kept an eye on the horde and waited for about ten seconds. None of the Shamblers veered off from the group to follow them—they were all focused on me.

Lucky me.

"Guess I'm Mr. Popular tonight," I said, heading west before I cut back downtown. I made sure Grim Whisper was tight in my holster and Peaches was close to my side, before I started a slow jog down 20th.

My first step was met with a fist that launched me across the street.

Peaches growled and pounced, only to be swatted away in the opposite direction. I didn't even sense an energy signature until the figure drew close. Even then it was a muted thing, almost non-existent.

"You dropped a building on me," the voice said. "I'm

going to make sure you feel pain before you die, Marked of Kali."

I peered up at the figure, shook my head and waited for my vision to clear as the stars stopped dancing. This poison was really making things difficult.

A woman approached, dressed in combat armor that seemed to be made of dark red silk. Every square inch of her clothing was covered in softly glowing orange runes that slowly and rhythmically pulsed and shifted, except for an area on her left side where I saw the outline of a rose.

It could only be one person with an opening like that.

Like I said, exceptional detection skills.

She was good. I didn't even sense her energy signature. Either she was getting better, or my senses were becoming dulled. The latter theory didn't work, though, since my early detection hellhound had failed to warn me about her approach.

She was getting better, which was bad news.

My sight cleared and I got a better look at my attacker. I knew who it was before she stepped out of the shadows and into the middle of the street.

Dira.

A very upset, looking to dive into some serious maiming, Dira.

Talk about horrific timing, but I shouldn't have been surprised. This was exactly the kind of thing I would expect from Kali and her successors.

"Dira," I said, flexing and rubbing the jaw she had nearly disconnected from my face. "It's good to see you. How was London? Did you enjoy the Tate?"

"I'm glad you've retained your sense of humor," she said, crossing the street. "Imagine how humorous it will be when I carve your life from your body."

"Wow, right to the life carving?" I asked. "Hey, I hope you understand that dropping a building on you wasn't personal."

"Oh, I understand," she said. "I understand that you need to die."

I got to my feet and looked over her shoulder. The Shamblers were still two blocks away.

"Listen, this is really a bad time," I said. "Can we schedule our fight to the death when I finish dealing with the undead?"

"I told you I would be there when you made your mistake," she said, ignoring me. "You remained here alone. This will be your last mistake. I will take great pleasure in—"

"I know, I know," I said, raising a hand. "You'll take great pleasure in seeing my last breath, putting me out of my misery, all while inflicting mind-numbing pain upon me. Did I miss anything? You'll have to take a number. I really have my hands full right now."

"You dare mock me?"

"I dare when I'm dealing with undead and a Revenant that, like you, wants me dead," I said, pointing behind her. "Meet my new fan club. I feel like they need a name."

She took a step back and turned slowly as if expecting some kind of attack. Her jaw flexed as she saw the Shamblers.

"The Walking Dead?" I continued. "Hmm, that might get me in trouble. Maybe something like Strong's Dead Heads? What do you think?"

"They're...they're dead?" she asked, looking at the group of Shamblers. "What abomination is this?"

"No, actually, those are Shamblers," I corrected. "Abominations are larger and uglier. Think ogres, only undead."

Peaches padded to my side, entering shred-and-maim mode with a low growl.

<She wants to hurt you.>

<I know, but stay back. We can't fight here. The undead zombies are coming.>

<I can bite her and then she will not be able to follow.>

<No. No biting or anything. We don't have time. Get ready to blink away.>

"This is your doing?" she asked, still fixated on the Shamblers. "Why would you summon the dead?"

"Why would *I* summon the dead?" I asked in disbelief. "Do I look like I would be able to summon the dead, or anything else for that matter?"

"You *look* like a coward," she said. "You and your mage dropped a building on me rather than face an honorable death in combat. You prefer to lose your life cowering in fear, rather than facing death as a warrior."

The words stung, but I didn't have time to get into a philosophical debate about what it meant to have honor. I could argue that trying to take me out every chance she got lacked honor, but that would only piss her off further. She was already upset that we'd dropped the Tate on her.

"I'm not cowering," I said. "Right now, I'm planning a strategic retreat so those things don't have me for dinner."

"This won't take long," she said. "I will relieve you of further concerns."

She materialized her blade.

A *Bas Magus*, loosely translated as a mage-killer. It was a sleek, dangerous-looking weapon. The blade was a dark silver, tinged with blue and covered in white runes. It was similar to the *kamikira,* which was designed to kill gods.

I reached inward for Ebonsoul as she took a step forward, then stopped in her tracks, scrunching her face in disgust.

"You smell wrong," she said, staring at me. "What have you done?"

"First off, rude much?" I said. "Second, you don't hear me complaining about your questionable assassin fashion sense."

"I am a successor, not an assassin, and you smell of poison," she said, looking at me. "You would poison yourself to avoid facing me? The Marked of Kali should be immune to poison. This is another ruse."

She took another step forward as I bared my arms.

"No ruse," I said. "Normally I would agree with you on my invulnerability, but this time it's real. I really don't have time to dance with you. I'd love to, but can't."

She stared down at my arms. The black veins pulsed with violet energy. Surprisingly, I felt no pain, but I could feel the slowing down of my healing as a result of the poison.

It's getting worse.

"I cannot kill you in this condition," she said, mostly to herself. "There is no honor in killing a sick dog."

Actually, she probably *could* kill me in this condition, but it would cheapen my death in her honorable eyes. Win for me.

She absorbed her blade and stepped back.

"You may leave to heal," she continued. "Once recovered, I will find you and end your miserable life. There is nowhere you can run, and there is nowhere you can hide. Anywhere you go, I *will* find you."

"That just makes me feel all kinds of warm inside," I said. "Nice of you to let me get better, just so you could kill me."

"It is only just," she said, completely serious. "You will die with the honor befitting the Marked of Kali."

"You can't imagine how comforting it is to have you uphold the tradition of how I should die," I said. "Since your calendar just cleared up, you want to lend me a hand with the zombies?"

The Shamblers were only a block away now.

"No," she said, glancing at the horde. "If this insignificant threat can kill you, then you never deserved to be the Marked of Kali. Consider this an opportunity to prove yourself worthy to die by my hand."

"Because *that's* my priority," I said. "Making sure I meet your standards of future victim."

"I understand that it isn't your priority," she said, "but it should be."

"I suggest you don't let them get ahold of you," I said. "They really like to reach out and touch you. If they do, you will be the one facing death."

She turned and started walking away.

"You will live to see another sunrise," she said, fading into the night. "Enjoy the time you have left."

"You could've offered to stick around and fight them at the very least," I called out into the night. "Hello? Incoming undead horde?"

No response.

"Let's go, boy. No need to blink—we need to lead the Shamblers further away."

Peaches rumbled and matched my pace as we ran west on 20th Street.

TWENTY-ONE

I had an idea as we arrived on Ninth Avenue.

<*Let's take them down here.*>

I pointed down Ninth.

<*I go where you go.*>

<*When I tell you, I need you to stay back.*>

<*I go where you go.*>

He said that more forcefully.

<*What's going on? You sound worried.*>

<*We are bondmates and you smell bad.*>

I knew he was referring to the poison in my system, but I wasn't going to get into it with him at the moment. He'd probably threaten me with a good tongue-lashing, and I wasn't in the mood for a slobber bath, so I tried deflection as we headed down Ninth at a quick pace.

<*Hey, I showered this morning.*>

<*Your insides still smell bad. Did you wash well?*>

<*I've been poisoned.*>

<*If you ate enough meat, you would not be poisoned.*>

<*Meat is not the solution to everything, you know. Maybe in hell-*

hound world, but not out here where undead creatures are trying to kill you.>

<You don't have to be scared. I am here. I will protect you. Even if you smell, you are still my bondmate.>

I wasn't scared. Well, maybe a little. Starring in your own personal zombie movie sounds fun for all of two seconds until you realize that it's a killer role, emphasis on killer.

<Do I say anything when you have sausage breath? No, I don't.>

<My breath smells strong.>

<You're not kidding there. Let's go.>

<Where are we going?>

<We're going to get rid of these Shamblers, and hopefully weaken their leader.>

This wasn't my best idea, but the way the night was going, it was par for the course. We were heading back to the only place that could blow these Shamblers to bits.

The Randy Rump.

Shamblers weren't exactly aware.

I understood that they were only executing what they were designed to do. It meant that they would follow me blindly until they caught up and siphoned my life force...and died, or re-died, trying.

The defenses of the Randy Rump were active. I remembered Monty's words: Only the backroom would survive the blast. Everything else would be rubble.

We arrived at the Rump a few minutes later.

The Shamblers were still moving slow, but their movements were less jerky. They seemed to be coordinating and moving more like a unit. I also noticed that the group seemed to be getting larger. At first, I thought it was the shadows playing tricks with my vision, when I realized the blue glow was stronger than it had been even ten minutes ago.

The group was definitely getting larger.

Some of the ones in the front were moving with purpose,

heading in my direction. One in particular gave off a brighter blue glow than the others around it. That one really began to pick up the pace and closed the distance.

"Well, shit," I said, drawing Grim Whisper as it approached. "That's not good."

I stepped inside the Randy Rump and made my way around the debris to the massive back room door. The fast Shambler remained outside for now, staring at me.

"Sssurrender," it said the emphasis on the first syllable and extending the first letter until it was a hiss. "You have no essscape."

Since when did they start speaking?

"I swear, if this thing starts demanding the precious, I'll shoot it on principle alone," I said, mostly to myself. "Go away, Smeagol. I'm busy."

"We will feed on you, cursssed one," it said, moving closer to the destroyed entrance. I could hear his friends coming down the street. "We will feed our massster."

"Sorry, I'm not on the menu today!" I called out as I approached the Buloke door to the backroom. "Your dinner plans are going to be canceled."

I pressed several runes out of sequence. I figured the defenses were designed to prevent any tampering with the door. Even though I wasn't a mage, I let power flow through me as I touched the runic defense.

The runes on the door reacted, glowing bright red with each rune I touched. Bright red meant the defenses were activating, or at least I hoped so. I had a few more runes left in the sequence, but I needed the Shamblers closer if I was going to start this party the right way.

"Simon Strong," the Shambler said, this time with no hissing. "This is futile. You have lost."

"Shit," I said, turning slowly. "You've lost your lisp. That you, Fel Sepsis?"

The Shambler took several steps forward as I tightened my grip on Grim Whisper.

"You insignificant speck of dust," Fel said. "You would mock a god?"

"Hmm, give me a moment," I said, and paused. "Yep. Especially one who specializes in reanimating his followers. What's the matter? You can't convince the living to follow you? You have to force them after they're dead?"

"Brave words for someone who wields no power. You are not a mage. You cannot open that door," Fel-Shambler said. "This ruin will be your grave."

"I'm getting really tired of people telling me the obvious," I said. "Mages are overrated. Most of the ones I know walk around with overinflated egos just because they can wiggle their fingers and make sparkles. Pfft, big deal."

"I can raise the dead to serve me," Fel said menacingly. "I have the power of a god."

"Ah, I see," I said with a nod. "Tonight's entertainment is going to be delusion with a side of major megalomania."

"You stupid excuse of a human. You have no—"

I aimed Grim Whisper and fired, removing Fel-Shambler's head. It fell to the ground and burst to dust a second later. Another Shambler stepped into view.

"That...hurt my feelings," I said as the second Shambler approached. "No need to resort to insults. Do you see me bringing up how you were outmaneuvered and sealed behind a door, because you believed your own hype? No, you do not."

"Resistance is futile," it said. "Do you understand your situation now?"

"Tell me, how did Orethe manage to steal five hundred mages from right under your nose?" I asked. "That must've stung. You were *so close* and then, poof, gone. Sent to your room."

The Shambler vibrated with rage. For a moment, I thought it was going to shake itself apart.

"You know nothing," Fel said. "I trusted her and she betrayed me. She robbed me of...everything. I shall not be so foolish this time. Now the truth must be apparent. Resistance truly is—"

"Fuck me," I said, shooting the second Shambler to dust. "I'm not dying to the zombie Borg tonight."

A third Shambler replaced the one I just dusted.

"My horde is growing," Fel said. "Don't you sense it? This city is replete with death. I grow stronger by the hour. Soon, I will have my Abominations breach the morgues and this city will fall. Orethe and Mage Montague will be powerless to stop me. You will all be my slaves."

"Morgues?" I said. "What morgues?"

The Shambler spasmed and exploded.

Another Shambler stepped forward.

"I'm guessing that was the wrong question?"

More of the Shamblers filled the street outside the Randy Rump. It was beginning to get crowded out there. Peaches growled next to me but stayed back. If this plan didn't work, this night was going to go from bad to horrendous in a hurry.

"Beneath the facility you call Haven, lies a morgue."

A supernatural morgue.

"One you can't reach," I said. "That place is a fortress. Your Abominations will be dust before they get in there."

"This would be true if they attempted a frontal assault," he said. "Fortunately, this is a city of tunnels and underground passages. I will conquer the first morgue, increase my strength, and then make my way to the true prize."

The Fel-Shambler started laughing as it slowly dawned on me. It was disgusting to watch and horrific to hear. Nothing dead should be able to laugh like that.

I aimed Grim Whisper and removed the Shambler and the laugh from existence. Another Shambler stepped forward.

"It truly is a shame," Shambler number five said. "You will soon be feeding me, while your friends fall to my Abominations."

The street was beyond packed with Shamblers now. They all stood still, waiting. The sight was creepy and unnerving at the same time. They effectively blocked the front of the Rump, eliminating any exit I may have had.

I couldn't leave now even if I wanted to. Not without cutting through hundreds of Shamblers. I didn't have enough ammo for what I was looking at, and using Ebonsoul would get me swarmed in seconds.

I needed to get to Monty and Orethe. They were walking into a trap.

"We're going to agree to disagree," I said, pressing the last set of runes. I grabbed Peaches around the neck with my free hand and activated my dawnward. The violet dome formed around us. "By the way, I was never trying to *open* the door."

The runes on the door began to pulse red as the energy around the Randy Rump surged. All of the runes in the Rump took on a red glow. For a few seconds, they all pulsed in sync, and then they stopped pulsing, increasing in intensity.

"Your ploy was useless," the Shambler said, moving forward into the Rump. "You have only delayed the inevitable. It is time for you to—"

A moment later, the Randy Rump exploded.

TWENTY-TWO

The dawnward took the brunt of the blast.

I took the rest.

A wave of red energy rushed forward in every direction, blasting everything in its path. It obliterated walls, floors, furniture, and the cars parked on the street.

It tore through the concrete and melted the asphalt. The Shamblers had no chance.

The wave of energy washed over the Shamblers, obliterating everything it touched and converting them to dust. For a few moments, I breathed a sigh of relief that my plan had worked.

Then Peaches whined next to my leg.

The violet dome of the dawnward was gradually disappearing. The red defense wave was devouring that, too.

<*Can you blink us out of here?*>

<*No. There is too much energy in the air. We would get lost. You could get hurt.*>

<*Get ready. That red wave is going to bring down the dawnward and launch...*>

The dawnward collapsed.

Peaches jumped in front of me as the red energy wave blasted us out of the Rump. We sailed out of the Rump and landed in the street with several bounces.

Peaches recovered before I did, and locked his jaws on my arm, stopping me before I smashed into a wall.

<Thanks, boy. At least we got rid of all those...>

Another whine followed with a low growl.

I turned in the direction my hellhound was facing.

All the defenses had done was cut a wide swath through the growing horde of Shamblers. Most of them were gone, but I could see where more were forming.

"This Fel is really starting to get on my nerves," I said, getting to my feet. "We need to find a way to destroy them before they go after the people in the city, and I don't have that kind of firepower."

Peaches looked up and gave off a low rumble.

"What now?" I said. "Flying Shamblers?"

Three figures landed in the streets near us.

If these were the upgrades, we were done.

One of the figures stepped out of the darkness and into the light—I recognized her immediately.

Vi.

She was flanked by two more Valkyries. Both of them dwarfed her as they stepped closer.

"Hades sends his regards," Vi said with a nod. "This is Maul"—she motioned to her right—"and Braun."

Maul held a flaming black hammer that was as long as I was tall, and Braun looked like she could bench press the gym as a warm up. She wore enormous black gauntlets covered in spikes.

"Now that is some exceptional destruction," Maul said approvingly. "Did you do this, Strong?"

"No—well, yes. It was the defenses of the Randy Rump that did most of the damage."

"Where is this Randy Rump you speak of?" Braun asked. "I only see devastation."

"Well, it was over there," I said, pointing to the crater that used to be the Rump. "Now it's gone."

"Outstanding," Braun said, clapping me on the shoulder. "You removed an entire edifice on your own. Good work for a small human. You should be proud of what you have done. Own it. This is good destruction."

I stared from Maul to Braun in disbelief before turning to Vi.

"I'm really glad to see you," I said, thankful they weren't some kind of flying Shambler mutation. "I managed to get many of them, but they're worse than roaches. They keep coming back."

Maul nodded.

"The draugar are foul, disgusting creatures," Maul said, hefting the hammer off her shoulder. "We will dispose of them."

"Draugar?" I asked. "What are draugar?"

"Those disgusting undead creatures you see forming in the street," Maul said, adjusting her hammer. "That is what we call them."

I looked at Braun.

"You intend to get close to them?" I asked, concerned. "They're siphons. Getting close may be a bad idea."

"Not a problem," Braun said, making a pair of fists and cracking her knuckles at the same time. "They won't touch me."

"I don't see how that's going to—"

Braun ran up to the closest group of forming Shamblers and drove a fist into the ground. A wave of black energy rushed out from where she stood in a large circle of kinetic and eldritch power.

The ground shook, knocking the Shamblers back as the

black wave of energy raced out and enveloped them. In seconds, the blue glow of the undead was gone.

Braun walked back to where we stood.

"They won't touch me," Braun said again with a wide grin. "Come, Maul, let's make quick work of this. Draugar are nothing for us."

Maul nodded.

"This is almost beneath us, Virago," Maul said, turning to Vi. "We should be facing the source of this madness. I haven't killed a necromancer in ages."

"That is not for us to decide," Vi said. "Hades wants us here, so we are here. Please begin dispatching the undead."

Maul and Braun raced off into the street and began obliterating Shamblers. Maul brought her hammer down, sending a wave of black flame up the street. It devoured every Shambler it encountered.

"That's impressive," I said. "Is this the Midnight Echelon?"

"Part of it," Vi said, observing the other two in action. "This is a stopgap measure. They will tire eventually. You need to address Fel Sephtis."

"Wouldn't it be better if we *all* addressed Fel, with extreme force?" I asked, knowing her answer. "That would get this done in no time flat."

"That falls to you, Mage Montague, and Orethe," she said. "This is our part, as decreed by Hades and the Allfather."

"Right, and you aren't known for breaking decrees, are you?"

"Not even once," she said, drawing her blade. Black smoke wafted up from the blade into the night. "You are needed elsewhere, Strong, Bondmate of the Mighty Hellhound Peaches. We will deal with the draugar—you remove the head of the snake."

"Mighty Peaches?" I asked. "Are we talking about the same hellhound?"

"How many scions of Cerberus do you know?" she asked.

"Just this one."

"Have you heard of any other hellhound named Peaches?"

"No, never."

"Then I have spoken true," she said, rubbing my hellhound's massive head as he stood perfectly still and a little taller. "He is a Mighty Hellhound."

"I know this," I said. "I'm just curious how *you* know this?"

"This is not the time for idle talk," she said. "There is killing to be done. Go do it."

She ran off after Maul and Braun.

This was going to be a problem.

<Did you hear? Did you hear what she called me? The Mighty Peaches.>

<I heard. Can you blink us to Monty, Oh Mighty One?>

He sniffed the air and chuffed.

<I can get close, but there is something in the way.>

<Close is good. Let's do it.>

<Stand near me, bondmate of the Mighty Peaches. I will take you where you need to go.>

I sighed. This Mighty Peaches thing was going to be an issue.

He gave off a low rumble and barked.

The next moment, we had left the Valkyries and the destruction of the Shamblers behind.

TWENTY-THREE

We arrived a few blocks away from the New York City Mortuary.

I turned to see Monty blasting Shamblers to oblivion, with Orethe weaving in and out of their proximity in a deadly dance of destruction.

Everywhere she turned, Shamblers erupted into dust.

"Good of you to join us," Monty said as he unleashed a barrage of violet orbs. "We seem to have encountered some resistance."

I drew Grim Whisper and finished off the remaining Shamblers.

"Is Haven connected to the Mortuary?" I asked, hoping the answer was no. "Tell me it isn't."

"Not to my knowledge," Monty said. "I could be wrong."

"I really hope you aren't," I said, pulling out my phone and dialing Roxanne. "Pick up, pick up."

The call went to voice mail and I hung up.

"She did say she was going underground," Monty said, concerned. "Why do you ask?"

"Fel said he was going to take down the Mortuary and then take the morgue in Haven."

"Fel said?" Orethe asked quickly. "You spoke to Fel?"

"Well, his Shamblers—"

"Stop," she said. "It wasn't an Abomination? Are you certain?"

"Yes," I said, annoyed. "There's a huge difference between a Shambler and an Abomination—literally."

"No," Orethe said as her expression became grim. "He's here."

"What exactly does that mean? He's here? Here, as in using his Abominations and Shamblers as puppets? Or here, as in we're going to bump into him soon?"

"The latter," she said. "What did this Shambler say, exactly?"

"Well, it was actually a conversation over five Shamblers and—"

"The message, Simon," Monty said, glancing at the exasperated Orethe, who was continuing to stare at me. "What did Fel say?"

"He specifically said he was going to take over the *morgues*—plural," I said. "He was referring to the Mortuary *and* Haven."

"How could he?" Monty said. "They are in separate facilities. Haven would require an army to penetrate while locked down."

"Not if they are connected underground," I said, holding up a finger. "I know who to call. One sec."

I pressed another number.

The call connected in a few seconds.

"Zombies!" said a panicked voice, as I pulled the phone away from my ear. "They're everywhere! Get safe, Strong…go, go, go!"

"Hello, Hack," I said when he was done and calmed down a bit. "I need your help."

"I'm not going to fight zombies, sorry, no can do," he said, breathing hard. "They eat your brains! Did you know? Your brains! I need my brain—it's my best feature."

"Your brain is safe," I said. "I don't need you to fight them, I need information on old architectural plans."

"Oh, that I can do," he said, his voice suddenly calm. "Where and what?"

I shook my head. Hack was certifiable.

"The New York City Mortuary. Is it connected to Haven?"

"Give me a sec," he said as I heard the tapping of keys. Then, "Not anymore."

"Not *anymore*?" I said. "But they were?"

"Yes, about a century ago," he said. "Haven used to transport its deceased to the Mortuary using underground railway tunnels for disposal. Makes sense. You don't want to transport dead bodies through the streets. It was a major health hazard."

"Shit," I said. "Can you give me access points to these tunnels?"

"Only two access points left. The rest have been sealed or constructed over," he said. "Hold on. Sent them to you. Actually, you're close to one of the access points right now; it's about two blocks over and looks like an old subway ventilation shaft. Image and location sent."

"Thanks, Hack, I owe you," I said, ending the call and looking at Monty. "We need to get there now."

I led the way to the shaft.

"What happened to the Shamblers following you?" Orethe asked. "You destroyed them?"

"Well, I destroyed a large group of them, but Fel is drawing energy from the city itself," I said. "Something about the city being replete with death? There are more on the streets."

"If he's using Shamblers to communicate, he's grown stronger," she said as we moved. "I feared this would happen."

"Feared what would happen?"

"Fel can draw ambient energy from an area if there has been enough death," she answered. "That's why I thought he would focus on the morgues, but this city...this city is filled with death. It permeates its very essence."

"You didn't think this would be important to share? You know, earlier?"

"I didn't think he had enough power," she said. "He was using the Shamblers and Abominations but only communicating through the Abominations."

"He was pretending to be weaker than he really was," Monty said. "It was a deception. Simon, how did you handle the Shamblers? You said you destroyed a part of them. What happened to the rest?"

"Nightwing happened," I said. "Hades sent them to assist in getting rid of the rest. I suggested they come help deal with Fel."

"I'm certain they declined," Monty said. "It would be against their instructions."

"Decree," I clarified. "It was decreed they could only deal with the Shamblers, or draugar, as they call them."

"Draugar, of course," Monty said as we arrived at the ventilation shaft. "That makes sense. It's the only way he could send the Dark Valkyries."

"I'm glad it makes sense to someone," I said. "You should've seen those Dark Valkyries in action. We could have used them against Fel."

"It seems Hades can't be involved directly," Monty said. "Valkyries, even dark ones, give him plausible deniability, but they can't be seen attacking Fel, as it would implicate…other entities. There's a deeper plan in play here."

"You think?" I said, pulling out my phone and looking at the site plans Hack had sent me. "Would be nice to know what that plan is exactly."

"Is this it?" Monty asked as he stood in front of the shaft door and formed a bright red orb. "This is the entrance?"

"Yes. According to these plans, there's a tunnel that runs between Haven and the Mortuary, down this shaft."

"Then we go down there and end Fel before he can get to Haven," Orethe said. "If he's drawing from the ambient energy, he's not using an Abomination or a Shambler—he's down there."

"I thought he couldn't use all of his ability until he eliminated me and Monty," I asked as I stepped back from the vent shaft door. "How is he doing this?"

"You're operating under a misconception," she said. "This is Fel using a fraction of his ability. If he manages to kill you both, we're all dead."

"You're serious?" I said.

"Dead serious," she said. "I never developed a sense of humor."

"Seems to be a trend with magic users," I said, glancing at Monty. "Monty, let's do this."

He unleashed the red orb.

"Stand back," he said. "This will not be an elegant solution, but time is of the essence."

The orb collided with the door, punching through the thick metal and creating a large opening. Orethe went first, and Monty followed in after her. I brought up the rear with Peaches by my side.

I noticed the thickness of the door as we entered.

"Why make the doors so thick?" I asked. "Were they afraid the dead were going to escape?"

"It was an added security measure," Monty said as we descended a long flight of stairs. "Designed mostly to prevent theft."

"Who would want to steal dead—? Nevermind."

"You didn't specify how you eliminated the Shamblers," Monty said. "How did you do it? To my knowledge, you don't possess that type of burst damage, although at Scola Tower you did exhibit some potential. Still, we are not in proximity to a place of power. How did you pull it off?"

I noticed that mage brains defaulted to professor mode when confronted with something they couldn't understand. I could leave Monty alone and he would have a conversation with himself, trying to figure out how I dispatched the Shamblers.

I figured I'd save him the time and brainpower.

"I used the Randy Rump. Well, what used to be the Randy Rump."

"You utilized the defenses of the Rump?" he asked, surprised. "Ingenious and dangerous. How much of the Rump was left?"

"Let's just say that the next sign will have to say: *The New and Improved Randy Rump*," I answered. "Right now it's a Randy Rump crater, except for the back room. That managed to survive."

"Good thing," he said. "If the runes on that door failed, it wouldn't have been just the Rump. There would have been a crater the size of several blocks in diameter."

I stared at the back of his head.

"A heads up would've been nice."

"How *did* you manage to survive?" he asked. "That blast should have obliterated you, or at the very least broken every bone in your body. The kinetic component of the defenses was designed to forcefully expel any attacker, followed up with an energy component that should have melted you in place."

"Do you sit down and think these things up?"

"Yes, actually," he said. "How did you survive unscathed?"

"Dawnward took most of the blast," I said. "It failed after a few seconds and we were launched across the street. Peaches stopped me from becoming street pizza."

"Fascinating," he said, glancing at Peaches. "Your creature is quite impressive in action. We may have to run some tests on him to see the levels of his tolerances. I'd like to know the upper limits of his indestructibility."

"How about no?" I said. "We are not blowing him up to see how much he can take."

"It's just a suggestion," he said. "Empirical evidence always surpasses theory."

"We're going to stick with hellhound theory on this one," I said as we reached the bottom of the stairs. "This looks like it."

We arrived at the wide railway tunnel, which reminded me of the subway, except there was only one set of tracks and the tunnel was poorly lit. Monty stepped close to one of the walls and read a sign.

"That way leads to the Mortuary," he said, pointing down one end of the tunnel. "I have to assume Haven is in the opposite direction."

"Can you sense where Fel is?" I asked Orethe. "I know he said he would go for the easy target first, but we can't trust anything he says."

She closed her eyes and focused. After a few deep breaths, she pointed toward the Mortuary.

"He's in that direction."

"Are you sure?" I asked. "If we head to the Mortuary and he's at Haven, we won't be able to get to him in time."

"I'm sure. You don't trust my judgment?"

"It's not a matter of trusting your judgment," I said. "Fel works with deception. He could be using a fake energy signature, or something like that. He tricked us all into thinking he was weak...*all* of us."

"Good point," she said. "Why don't you ask them where Fel is?"

She pointed down the tunnel.

"Ask who? Oh, shit."

Three Abominations were headed our way from the direction of the Mortuary.

TWENTY-FOUR

"This is definitely an unwelcome committee," I said, drawing Grim Whisper. "Fine, Fel is that way. How do we get past them?"

"Put your gun away—it won't do anything," she said. "Except maybe anger them further."

I holstered Grim Whisper.

"Can you enhance your magic-missile blast?" she said, forming a yellow orb as she moved to approach the Abominations. "Like the one you used before, with your Ebonsoul?"

"I don't know," I said. "I think I got lucky."

"You need to find that luck again," she said. "Mage Montague, an energy lattice to delay them would be ideal. Preferably one that inflicts pain, so as to get their attention."

Monty nodded and gestured, forming a golden lattice of energy that raced down the tunnel, expanding as it went until it blocked the entire thing. It stopped about fifty feet away.

The Abominations kept coming.

"According to the plans Hack sent me, the Mortuary is half a mile in that direction, past the Abominations," I said. "Haven is about the same distance behind us."

A roar filled the tunnel, grabbing our attention. One of the Abominations had tried to get past the lattice. It failed, and had lost an arm in the process.

"That is an effective lattice," Orethe said, heading to the Abominations. She still held her orb. She whispered some words over it and placed a finger on its surface before releasing it. "Pay attention, Simon."

The orb bobbed in the air, still glowing bright yellow. A few seconds passed before I noticed the surface began to change. Black runes swirled over the surface of the orb, transforming it until the yellow had completely disappeared.

Orethe nodded and tapped the orb with a finger.

It bobbed one more time and then took off, trailing yellow light in its wake.

"What the—?"

"Avert your gaze," she said, turning her face to one side. "That one packs quite a punch."

I followed her instructions, turning my face to the side. I saw Monty do the same. Only Peaches kept his gazed fixed on the Abominations. I figured he would be fine; somehow, I didn't think he would be in danger of being blinded. Firing beams out of his eyes probably made them fairly blast-proof.

The orb impacted and turned the darkness of the tunnel into a summer afternoon of brightness. I didn't feel heat coming from the light, but when I turned, the Abominations had shrunk to wrinkled husks of their former selves.

"What was that?" I asked, surprised. "You raisined them."

"Close," she said. "Instead of removing all liquid from their bodies, that orb removes the energy that drives them by causing a cascade that expends it. You will learn this one day, but not today."

"A temporal accelerator," Monty said, intrigued. "You forced them to burn through their energy instantly."

"Won't Fel just give them more?" I asked. "It's not like they're—"

Before I could continue, she unleashed a black-and-golden blast that cut through the lattice and Abominations, reverting them to dust.

"I'm sorry?" she said. "You were saying?"

"Can that work on Fel?"

"No," she said, shaking her head and moving forward. "Abominations are simple, dangerous constructs of energy and dead flesh. It's simple to disrupt what's holding them together. Fel is a Revenant. He used to be human—once. He will be much harder to eliminate."

"Right. Why would I even imagine it would be that easy?" I said. "Nothing in my life is ever that easy."

"Get used to it," she said. "Fel is ahead."

We arrived at a large, rune-covered steel door.

"These runes are recent," Monty said, peering at the door. "I can't decipher them. Orethe?"

"Death runes," she said. "Basically, the function is in the name. One moment."

"I'm really starting to dislike Fel at this point," I said. "Death runes? Really?"

"I would imagine that if he could create a semblance of life through necromancy," Monty said, examining the runes from a distance, "death would be the same."

"Just inverted," Orethe added. "And permanent."

Monty glanced at Orethe, who moved closer to the steel door.

"Those runes look formidable," he said. "Can you read them?"

"Don't need to."

"What?" I asked shocked. "You're going to guess?"

I recalled that I had used the same strategy for the door

at the Randy Rump, but I got lucky. I didn't think I was that lucky that the same method would work twice without blowing us to atoms.

"I'm not going through the runes," she said. "That would take too long."

"But you're going to get through that door?" I asked. "How? Convince him to open it for you?"

"Something like that," she said. "Once I do, we'll be facing Fel. No more Shambler or Abomination proxies, except as fodder to distract us."

"How strong is he now?" I asked, not being able to sense Fel's energy signature. "Can you tell?"

"Strong enough to pose a significant threat," she said, flexing the muscles in her jaw. "We can't let him get to the other morgue. Even if it means our lives. Do you both understand? We end him here."

"Understood," I said as Monty nodded. "We end him here."

Orethe placed one hand on the door and the other on her focus. The tunnel lit up with yellow light, accented with streaks of violet.

"Won't that, I don't know—kill her?" I asked Monty, who was examining the process with narrowed eyes. "She can touch death runes without it affecting her?"

"She's not disrupting the integrity of the runes," he said, lowering his voice. "She's undoing...the door? Extraordinary."

He was right. The door began to show signs of rust and aging as metal began to flake off its surface. Holes began to appear after half a minute, and two minutes later there was no door. The runes vanished as the remaining parts of the door crumbled to dust.

"No door, no runes, no death," she said. "Let's go. From this point forward, Fel won't hold back. Be ready."

She stepped through the doorway.

"He's been holding back?" I asked as we followed. "Are you sure we can't call in for backup?"

Monty nodded as we followed her into the darkness.

TWENTY-FIVE

The Mortuary was immense.

It made sense.

This place was designed to hold the dead for an enormous city. As the mortuary for the City, the Office of the Chief Medical Examiner took custody of all remains. This included all unidentified or unclaimed remains throughout the five boroughs of New York City.

In other words, Fel was looking at a huge power upgrade by getting in here. Even as bad as that was, getting into Haven would be worse. Most of the remains in their morgue had supernatural origins. If Fel fed off of those, we were done.

All he needed to do was kill me and Monty first.

"No more strange rituals," I said as we entered the morgue. "If York hadn't hit us with that unorthodox Stormblood ritual—"

"We'd probably be in a worse situation right now," Monty finished. "York, in his own way, helped us."

I looked around the morgue.

It was a negative-temperature morgue, which meant the

place was cold, frigid even. The walls were lined with front-loading refrigerated cabinets, stacking four bodies each.

The center of the floor was mostly bare, except for some tables which I assumed that were used to discover cause of death by the medical examiners.

Four enormous circular columns stood equally spaced around the room. The walls and floor were an off-white medical tile, the kind only seen in horror movies. The only features in the floor were large, round floor drains every six to eight feet. Other than that, the room was bare.

"Helped us?" I said. "We're standing in a room surrounded by dead bodies facing off against a necromancer. A *undead necromancer*. This is called a worst-case scenario. I don't see a worse situation. Unless we somehow joined them—that would be a worse situation."

"That *would* make the situation dire," Monty said. "Let's not burn that bridge until we cross it. How about we focus on the task at hand? We need to find Fel and put an end to this."

"We won't have to look far," Orethe said, turning slowly. "I think he's found us."

A figure stood near the wall behind us.

We turned and were faced with Fel Sephtis.

"Indeed," he said, dryly. "It is my pleasure to finally meet you all, in the flesh, so to speak."

Fel wore a bespoke black Zegna suit, with a blood-red shirt and a dark gray, almost black, tie. He looked like a mage fresh off the runway from some Italian fashion show.

He wore his salt-and-pepper hair long, reminding me a bit of Monty and his only unkempt feature. I glanced from Fel to Monty, and then back to Fel.

"Don't even say it," Monty said. "He looks nothing like me."

"You have to admit, there's a certain mageyness to the

look," I said, then turned to Fel. "You're well dressed for someone who's been trapped behind a seal."

"*Vestis virum facit*," Fel said, staring at me. "Yours speak volumes."

"Translation?" I asked, glancing at Monty. "My Latin is rusty."

"Clothes make the man," Monty said. "Educated and pretentious."

"Typical magic user, then," I said, giving Fel a once over. "I'm not reading much of an energy signature. We can take him."

"That would be a mistake," Orethe said. "He's not entirely human."

"You would do well to heed her words," Fel said. "Well, I'd like to say this has been pleasant, but it hasn't. It was good seeing you again, Orethe. I really do hate to have to kill you, but I'm sure you understand. This isn't personal."

"I find it fitting you chose a morgue to meet us in," Orethe said, shaking out her hands. "You're going to die here."

"Wrong," Fel said, slashing the air with an arm. "They were too lenient with you, letting you live. I will make sure you are finished this time."

A blue arc of energy raced through the air at us.

I dropped to the floor, letting it slice the space above me. I felt the heat radiate from the arc as it passed overhead, searing the air as it crossed the room. I moved to take cover behind one of the large columns.

Orethe raised a hand and bisected the arc, sending the two sections flying off in separate directions, cutting deep grooves into the walls. Monty slid over to the column where I was crouching.

"He's not using Abominations or Shamblers," Monty said, keeping his voice low as Orethe unleashed a blast at Fel, who deflected it away with a wave of his hand, blasting a nearby wall and showering the morgue with tile shrapnel. "We can make use of this."

I stared at Monty as if he had lost his mind.

"In what dimension do you think we have a chance in this fight?" I asked. "He's not using Shamblers or Abominations because he wants to kill us with his own hands."

"Or because he can't," Monty said. "We're inside a morgue. Why isn't he brimming with power? Plenty of dead bodies to use as fuel."

"Did you not see the arc of energy he casually threw our way?"

"I think he's reached his limit," Monty said. "We need to confront him and end this."

"And if you're wrong?"

"Then this will be one of our shortest fights ever," Monty said. "We're going to need to buy Orethe some time—I think she's weaker than she has let on. Can you get his attention while I see to her?"

"Attention-getting, I can do," I said. "Staying alive while the pissed-off necromancer tries to end me is not my idea of fun."

"I have every confidence in your ability to do both," Monty said. "Let your hellhound harass him as well. We need to create a large enough distraction."

"Got it," I said, glancing down at my amazing hellhound. "We'll keep him busy. Don't take too long—and you're going to want to use something to save your hearing. Let me brief him."

Monty nodded and gestured.

"Ready," Monty said. "On your signal."

<Hey, boy.>

<The bad man wants to hurt the lady. Can I bite him?>

<No, I want you to bark as loud as you can. Can you do that?>

<That would break your ears. I don't want to hurt you.>
<I'll be okay. Can you do it?>
<Yes.>
<Good. I'm going to get his attention, then you bark at him as loud as possible.>

I glanced at Monty, drew Grim Whisper and nodded as I stepped out from behind the column.

"Hey, Fel Sepsis," I said, firing my weapon. None of the rounds reached him. "I'm feeling a little left out. I thought you were here to kill me and Monty?"

I really hope you know what you're doing, Monty.

Fel looked my way for half a second, unleashing a barrage of small blue orbs in my direction, before returning his focus to Orethe. They crackled with energy as they raced at me. I took off at a dead run, diving behind another column—which the orbs punched holes through.

That doesn't look like he's low on power.

"Where are your minions?" I called out from behind the punctured column. "Let me guess, you have a union crew and they're all on break? Or is it that you haven't authorized overtime?"

Orethe had ducked behind another column with Monty beside her. She was in bad shape. Her face was cut and bloody, and one of her arms was hanging wrong. Monty was right. She wasn't going to last much longer at this pace.

"Strong?" Fel called out. "I'm going to enjoy draining you dry. Your life-force will elevate me to my full strength."

"You know what I think?" I said, and patted Peaches on the head. "I don't think you have any power left. Why aren't you siphoning the bodies around us? I think you overextended yourself."

<Now, boy. Go give him your loudest bark.>

Peaches blinked out as I stepped out into the open.

"So eager to die," Fel said, forming a blue orb of power.

"Your mage may have opened the door, but you...you will be responsible for ushering in the new age of my reign."

I raised Grim Whisper.

"Pointless," he said. "You will die where you sta—"

Peaches blinked in on Fel's blindside and barked. I materialized a dawnward and hoped it would hold.

It didn't.

The sound was a combination of a freight train crashing into a truck, during a thunderstorm, as half the planet exploded. The tiles in front of Peaches disintegrated.

All of the runes on his flanks lit up a bright red. The dawnward disappeared a second later. I moved behind the column to escape the incoming blast as it knocked me on my back.

The sound hit Fel squarely, launching him to the other side of the morgue floor and slamming him into the refrigerated cabinets, which dented inward from the sonic blast as Peaches let out a low growl, took a step and fell to his side, unconscious.

The high-pitched whine in my ears reached stratospheric levels as I touched one of my ears to see if I was bleeding.

On the other side of the floor, Fel finished his bouncing off the cabinets and crumpled to the floor. He was up a few seconds later.

Totally not fair. He should have been blasted to bits by that bark.

He looked wrecked.

His Zegna suit was in shreds. That made me smile. His face looked like it had been used as a punching bag for at least fifteen rounds by an angry Mike Tyson in his prime.

He also looked extremely upset.

"You insolent cur," he said, focusing on Peaches. "I will end you and then I will end your master."

Shit. Peaches was still out cold.

I stumbled to my feet.

I could sense the energy gathering from Fel's side of the floor, but the only thing I could focus on was my hellhound's body lying on the floor.

My last thought before the world erupted in an electrical blue was:

That energy signature doesn't feel like he's out of power.

I jumped the last few feet and intercepted the orb meant for my hellhound with my body. It blasted into my back and flung me to the side. I hit the cabinets shoulder first and heard the crack before I fell to the floor.

I was certain I had a few broken ribs, among other things. My arm decided it wasn't listening to my suggestions to move. Took me a moment to realize the broken clavicle may have had something to do with that.

I felt another burst of power, and then the pain politely throat-punched me with new waves of agony.

My body became a raging inferno as it dealt with the damage. I nearly passed out from the pain; only my fear for Peaches kept me conscious. I got to my feet, using the wall for support.

Monty raced over to where I stood and threw a shield over Peaches.

"Thanks," I said. "I think I have his attention now."

"We're ready," Monty said. "Are you in much pain?"

"Oh no, I always enjoy slamming into metal cabinets and breaking parts of myself," I snapped and then hissed as another wave of pain decided to crush my body. "What makes you ask?"

"If you can answer like that, it must not be too bad," Monty said, nodding to Orethe. "I have…a plan."

"For the record, your last plan sucked," I said—and then I noticed Fel was gone. "Where is he?"

"He ported to the tunnels," he said, his voice tight. "He's

heading to Haven. We can stop him, but it's going to be dicey."

"Dicey!" I nearly yelled. "You're worried about dicey? If he gets to Haven, we are dead. Forget about dicey!"

"Remember those words when the agony starts," Monty said, his voice low. "Orethe, we're ready to begin."

TWENTY-SIX

Orethe limped over to where I stood.

She looked about as bad as I felt.

"Whatever you're going to do, you better do it fast," I said. "Haven is a mile from here and we're losing time."

"Form your blade," she managed around a cut lip. "Form Ebonsoul."

"What is that going to do? Did you hear what I said? Fel is heading to Haven."

She slapped me across the face. Hard. Hard enough to get my attention.

"I need to you focus right now, Simon," she said. "Form Ebonsoul. Now."

Off to the side, Monty was treating Peaches with a flow of golden runes. My hellhound opened his eyes, shook his body, and padded over to where I stood, freshly slapped.

"Now, Simon, please," Orethe continued. "Like you said, we're losing time."

I reached for Ebonsoul and screamed. My body felt like my blood had been replaced with magma. Orethe grabbed me before I fell to the floor.

"It's only pain, Simon," she said through clenched teeth. "You should be intimately acquainted with it by now. Form the blade."

I reached for Ebonsoul as my vision blurred. The silver mist formed in my hand. I focused more and materialized the blade.

"Montague!" Orethe cried out. "Are you ready?"

"Nearly there," Monty said as he created a large green circle under us. "Are you certain this will take us to him?"

"If it doesn't, we'll all be dead and it won't matter anyway," she said. "Now for the heart of the matter."

She let me go and leaned me against a wall as my wobbly legs protested. Orethe grabbed the blade of Ebonsoul, cutting her hand in the process. With her other hand, she reached into her chest and ripped out her focus.

"What the hell are you doing?" I said, shocked. "That will kill you!"

She ignored me as she brought the glowing yellow focus from her chest to the hand holding Ebonsoul.

"I'm afraid you will have to find another teacher, Simon Strong," she said, and looked at Monty. "Now."

The world flashed green.

We reappeared in the tunnels.

In front of Fel.

"None of you have the decency to die," Fel said. "Once I reach Haven, I will make sure you spend several lifetimes suffering. I will—"

His eyes opened wide as Orethe leapt on him, crushing him in an embrace.

"Do it mage!" she called out as she unleashed her power. "Do it now. Use the elder rune."

Fel swiveled his head around to Monty.

"No! You can't!" he yelled. "I'm so close!"

Monty traced the lost elder blood rune, but this time he

added a portion I hadn't seen when we had faced Mahnes. Orethe's energy blazed in the tunnel. She glowed like a midday sun as Fel screamed. Her energy enveloped them both as he clawed at her arms.

They both suddenly began aging as a portal opened behind them.

"The last part, mage. Finish it," Orethe said. "Finish it, once and for all."

Monty hesitated for a second, looking into her eyes. She nodded.

He finished tracing the rune and the portal transformed into a whirlpool of violet-and-yellow energy.

"Simon, seek out Azrael," she said. "You have all of my knowledge in your blade; he can provide the instruction you will need. I leave you my home in Elysium. It is yours now, as my last disciple by right and decree."

"You don't know what you have done," Fel seethed. "You have destroyed everything."

"I've done what I should've done long ago," Orethe said. "There will be no sealing away this time, Fel. Necromancers have no place in this world. *We* have no place in this world."

"You will not rob me again," Fel said, struggling to get away, but too weak to put up a real fight. "You can't. I am a god. You can't kill me. You can't kill a god!"

"I already have."

She stepped back, causing them both to tumble into the portal and out of sight. Monty traced another rune, and the portal slowly vanished from sight.

"What did she do?" I asked, looking at the space where the portal was a moment ago. "Why?"

"She did what only she could do," Monty said, looking down the tunnel. "She was the only one who truly could have ended him."

I looked down at Ebonsoul.

Along the edge of the blade, if I held it at the right angle, I could see a yellow outline of energy. It felt heavier in my hands.

"All her knowledge is in this now?"

He nodded.

"Seems like a heavy burden," he said. "Are you going to reabsorb it?"

"I think I'd better," I said. "If I leave it out, it can get lost or stolen."

"Does it feel different to you?"

"Heavier," I said. "Still perfectly balanced, but heavier. There's an energy I don't recognize in it now."

"That makes sense," he said, looking at me. "Ready?"

I nodded and reabsorbed my weapon.

My brain exploded with images and flashes of violet, yellow, red, and black. The pressure on my head was immense, forcing me to fall to one knee. I pressed a hand against my temple.

"It's too much...too much," I said as I fell forward. "Too—"

The last thing I remembered before losing consciousness was the green flash of a teleportation circle.

TWENTY-SEVEN

"I can't believe you let him absorb it," I heard a familiar female voice say. "Do you understand the threat that blade poses now?"

"I didn't think—"

"No, Tristan, you didn't think," she said. "He's been poisoned, and now he has that thing inside of him. How will it react to his other bonds? I don't know. The priority is clearing the poison in his blood."

"Can't you do it?" Monty asked. "You're the best Haven has."

Monty was speaking to Roxanne—which meant I was in Haven. I tried to open my eyes, but only saw darkness.

"This poison is beyond me. You need a Crimson Phoenix."

"They were all killed."

"Not all," she said. "There are still some of them alive, somewhere."

"At least his healing has recovered," Monty said. "I know you're awake, Simon."

"What's going on?" I said. "Where's Peaches? Why is the room so dark?"

"He's right here, by your bed," Monty said as Peaches let out a low rumble. "It's not dark... It's complicated."

"Show him," Roxanne said. "Lift the bandages."

"Bandages?" I said, reaching for my face and feeling the bandages around my eyes. "Why am I wearing bandages? Am I blind? What happened?"

"You're not blind, and the bandages aren't for you," Monty said, stepping close. "They're for your nurses. You kept scaring them."

He pulled up a bandage and showed me a mirror.

Both my eyes gave off a red glow. I looked like Peaches right before he unleashed a baleful glare.

"Sweet," I said. "Can I fire beams like my hellhound too?"

"Sweet?" Roxanne said sternly. "No, not *sweet*. You have advanced runic poisoning. This glow in your eyes means your body is being corrupted. The closest we can determine is that the blade inside of you is reacting with the poison in your blood."

"What's going to happen? Am I going to go full Sith?"

"This is not a joke, Simon," she said. "I, we, don't know what's going on, or how this can affect you, either your body or your mind. Monty tells me you fought alongside a necromancer recently? Something about her passing on all of her knowledge to you through your blade?"

I nodded.

"She merged her focus with Ebonsoul. My brain nearly exploded when I reabsorbed it."

She glanced at Monty.

"You need to get your blood cleansed," she said after a pause. "I'm afraid of what could happen if this is left unchecked."

"Fine, let's start the procedure."

"We can't deal with something this advanced here," she said, shaking her head. "You should actually be dead by now. You need a specialist. You need the Crimson Phoenix."

"How do we find the Crimson Phoenix?"

"The best person to ask would be Ezra," she said. "If anyone knows, he would."

I nodded my head.

"How long have I been here?"

"Three days," she said. "It was fortunate you and Tristan were so close. It took us a day to stabilize you to the point your healing could take over. How do you feel?"

"Hungry," I said. "Can we order some Piero's? I could use a steak right now."

"No steak," Roxanne said, giving Monty a look of warning. "Salad and maybe some chicken. I'm serious."

"Even salad and chicken would be good right now," I said, suddenly remembering Jimmy and the Randy Rump. "Jimmy?"

"He and his charges are fine," Monty said. "The Randy Rump, or the crater formerly known as the Randy Rump, will require extensive renovations. The Council has mobilized due to its status as a neutral location. He is currently visiting his sleuth until the rebuilding is done."

"He's not really in the talking mood," Monty said. "I'll see what can be done about the new defenses."

"I'll have to make it up to him somehow when he gets back," I said. "What happened to Dex?"

"He's been here to see you while you recovered," Monty said and gave me a look that let me know there was more to discuss, but not here. Not in front of Roxanne. "Said he would be by to see you in a day or so."

I nodded as my stomach growled.

"I hope starvation isn't part of my recovery."

"Let's go get you some food."

"Something easy on his system," Roxanne said, giving him a stern look. "He's bonded to a hellhound, but he doesn't have the stomach of one."

"Understood," Monty said, heading for the door with Roxanne in tow. "Let me see what I can do. Be right back."

I looked out of the window into the night as the door whispered closed. My glowing red eyes reflected in the window. My wardrobe was going to have to include sunglasses, at least in the short term.

"Your eyes look radiant," a voice said from the corner. "Are you trying to mimic your hellhound?"

Hades.

"Thanks for the assist with the Nightwing," I said, because even though he was playing his god games, it never hurt to express gratitude when dealing with god-level power. "They make it out okay?"

"They're fine," Hades said. "They wanted to express their thanks to you for allowing them the opportunity to dispatch the draugar, as they call them."

"My pleasure," I said as Peaches padded over to Hades and nudged his hand. "He'll leave you alone for meat."

"I know," Hades said, creating a large sausage. Peaches delicately removed it from his hand and proceeded to devour it on the floor next to my bed. "Wait until he gets older. He'll eat you out of house and home."

"You knew what Orethe was planning, didn't you?"

"I had an idea—nothing concrete, but there were some indicators, yes," he said. "She defeated Fel with your help, left you her home as her one and only disciple or apprentice, and gave you her entire body of knowledge. I'd say you came out ahead. The knowledge you now possess is alone enough to make you a target."

"Because I didn't have enough targets on my back."

"I ask you to judge me by the enemies I have made,"

Hades said. "Roosevelt, I believe. You, Strong, have some exceptional enemies."

I stared at him for a few seconds, unwilling to say something that would get me blasted. I let out a long breath before speaking again.

"That knowledge almost exploded my brain," I said. "It's too much. I'm no necromancer."

"Orethe thought differently," he said. "She specifically asked for you. The bondmate to a hellhound. I was going to introduce you much later on. Your meeting her this early was...convenient."

Convenient, my ass. I knew he'd manipulated this situation somehow.

"This is too much information in my brain. I can barely think straight. I keep getting glimpses of things I don't understand."

"It's too much *right now*," he clarified. "You will get stronger and the information will open to you. TK and LD will visit soon; they have some insight into your new condition with your blade that should prove informative."

"Or explode my brain," I said. "I didn't want this."

"That's usually why it happens."

"What about my blood?" I asked. "Now I need to go see the Crimson Phoenix—except Fel wiped them all out."

"Not all of them," Hades said. "I believe you are acquainted with a certain, Quan?"

"She's White Phoenix."

"The sect the Crimson Phoenix was folded into."

"You know, I really dislike god games," I said, letting the frustration creep into my voice. "It aggravates me that gods play with humans like pawns."

"I'm aware of your feelings on the matter," he said. "If it's any consolation, I dislike them, too."

"Then why are you here?" I asked. "No offense, but every time we have a meet, it's a downward spiral of pain for me."

"I'm here because you don't need the Crimson Phoenix," he said. "They wouldn't help you anyway. In case you haven't noticed, your blood is tainted. You've been poisoned. Quan, however, may be of assistance."

"Really, wow, thanks for the newsflash," I said. "I hadn't considered that possibility. It's not like the glowing veins or my new baleful-glare hellhound eyes were clues or anything."

He smiled at me and I felt a little fear. It was never a good idea to anger a god—even one you were on good terms with.

"I know exactly what you need...that is, if you want to survive this poisoning intact," he said, steepling his fingers over his lips. "Are you interested?"

"In staying alive? All the way at the top of my to-do list."

"Who said the poisoning would kill you?"

"Isn't that what you're implying?"

"Not in the least," he said. "You could opt to let the poisoning run its course. I don't know what the outcome will be, but knowing you, I'm certain it will be interesting."

"You know what? I'm not really in the mood to find out. What do I need to do to deal with this?"

"What you need are blood lessons."

THE END

AUTHOR NOTES

Thank you for reading this story and jumping into the world of M&S with me.

Disclaimer: The Author Notes are written at the very end of the writing process. This section is not seen by the ART or my amazing Jeditor—Audrey. Any typos or errors following this disclaimer are mine and mine alone.

Book 16...wow.

I never thought we'd get this far and MS&P show no signs of slowing down. This was a different kind of story. Yes, there was major danger, (this won't be the last time they encounter the undead) but it was also a story of making peace with who you are and righting a wrong.

For the record, the endings of these books, though outlined, are not set in stone. I know this one seems like a cliffhanger, but really it's not. I do apologize for those who feel like I've left you hanging by your fingernails. If it's any consolation, I've started the next book (BLOOD LESSONS) and that should be out early September (soon™).

For past cliffhanger reference, please revisit the ending of

BLOOD IS THICKER. That ending earned me some serious side eye from readers. What can I say, I was young and inexperienced, daring, and willing to place myself in danger. I've matured a bit since then. These stories (and every story) ends when it needs to. If I try to write past what I consider the natural ending, it feels forced and (to me) degrades the feel of the entire story.

This is a little hard to explain, but I know when the ending is...the ending. Trust me, as a reader, I know what it's like to get near the ending of a book and say...hold on a sec, there's not enough book to wrap this all up...no. Don't you dare do it...no!

I promise not to keep you waiting too long.

Hold on a little longer.

So, now, Simon has a death blade. This will complicate his life to no end. Not only that, he's going to be perceived as a serious threat by several factions, many who will want that blade for their own plans and purposes. If Simon's life was interesting before, it's going to get catastrophic from here on out. Friends will become enemies, enemies will become uneasy allies, and new enemies will step into his life, threatening everything and everyone he holds dear.

Let's pivot for a second.

If you've read this far into the series, you know I don't usually retire neutral or good characters.

Orethe was an exception.

Someone had to die in this book, she wasn't entirely evil, but the potential for evil was there. In the end, she opted to bow out gracefully, by righting a wrong. It was the honorable thing to do, but it was still difficult to write. I really enjoyed her character (no I would never call Dame Judi Dench *old*. Perhaps, less young, but never *old*. I'm crazy, but not *that* crazy) and she was a pleasure to write. However, I knew from the moment she stepped into the story, her time was limited.

It was a new experience for me, writing a character I knew was going to die, and part of my brain tried to find ways of saving her. But in the end, if Fel was going to be taken out(and he really needed to be taken out), Orethe was going to do it and it had to be done her way.

Pivot back.

On Monty & Simon being abandoned to face Fel on their own.

They really weren't if you see what TK and LD did at Scola Tower and Hades later on with the Dark Valkyries, they were given plenty of assistance. In the next book, we'll see what happened to Dex and what he was doing when he went to visit the Morrigan first (no, not that...really? well okay maybe a little, this is Dex we're talking about) and why he didn't reappear in the story. It wasn't an oversight and ties into later books as well.

Overall, I really enjoyed writing this story for you. Every MS&P book flows when I write it and it's hard to keep them from becoming unruly, but out of all the series, this is the one that has the most balance of chaos and order, truly a strange paradox. This was a welcome change from finishing the Sepia Blue series (which was tough) and helped me get back into my storytelling stride.

Currently, I'm working on book 3 of the Gatekeepers (BLOOD BOND) and I'm noticing that there's a thread tying these books together. It's subtle, but if you narrow your eyes you can see it lol. I don't want to say too much about Porter and Bug because, spoilers. Also, I don't know if its going to go past three stories. We'll see how book 3 wraps up and then we can have a conversation if there should be more Porter & Bug stories.

In the next MS&P book, we'll have Simon learning more about Ebonsoul, Chi returning to his life, Quan giving him (painful) blood lessons, Dira trying to become the next of

Marked of Kali, and Verity trying to apprehend and erase Monty, things are going to be Monteguean in scope.

Fortunately, we have the Mighty Peaches to see us through—Meat is life!

Thank you again for jumping into this story with me!

SPECIAL MENTIONS

To Dolly: my rock, anchor, and inspiration. Thank you...always.

Larry & Tammy—The WOUF: Because even when you aren't there...you're there.

Larry & Tammy: For dialogue authenticity help...thank you for your insights.

Jim Ziller: For all the unnamed burial sites under NYC. They pose a particular danger if exploited.

Orlando A. Sanchez
www.orlandoasanchez.com

Orlando has been writing ever since his teens when he was immersed in creating scenarios for playing Dungeons and Dragons with his friends every weekend.

The worlds of his books are urban settings with a twist of the paranormal lurking just behind the scenes and with generous doses of magic, martial arts, and mayhem.

He currently resides in Queens, NY with his wife and children.

BITTEN PEACHES PUBLISHING

Thanks for Reading
If you enjoyed this book, would you please **leave a review** at the site you purchased it from? It doesn't have to be long... just a line or two would be fantastic and it would really help me out.

Bitten Peaches Publishing offers more books by this author. From science fiction & fantasy to adventure & mystery, we bring the best stories for adults and kids alike.

www.BittenPeachesPublishing.com

More books by Orlando A. Sanchez

The Warriors of the Way
The Karashihan*•The Spiritual Warriors•The Ascendants•The Fallen Warrior•The Warrior Ascendant•The Master Warrior

John Kane

The Deepest Cut*•Blur

Sepia Blue
The Last Dance*•Rise of the
Night•Sisters•Nightmare•Nameless•Demon

Chronicles of the Modern Mystics
The Dark Flame•A Dream of Ashes

Montague & Strong Detective Agency Novels
Tombyards & Butterflies•Full Moon Howl•Blood is Thicker•Silver Clouds Dirty Sky•Homecoming•Dragons & Demigods•Bullets & Blades•Hell Hath No Fury•Reaping Wind•The Golem•Dark Glass•Walking the Razor•Requiem•Divine Intervention•Revenant

Montague & Strong Detective Agency Stories
No God is Safe•The Date•The War Mage•A Proper Hellhound•The Perfect Cup•Saving Mr. K

Brew & Chew Adventures
Hellhound Blues

Night Warden Novels
Wander•ShadowStrut

Division 13
The Operative•The Magekiller

Blackjack Chronicles
The Dread Warlock

The Assassin's Apprentice
The Birth of Death

Gideon Shepherd Thrillers
Sheepdog

DAMNED
Aftermath

RULE OF THE COUNCIL
Blood Ascension•Blood Betrayal•Blood Rule

NYXIA WHITE
They Bite•They Rend•They Kill

IKER THE CLEANER
Iker the Unseen

TALES OF THE GATEKEEPERS
A Bullet Ballet•The Way of Bug•Blood Bond

*Books denoted with an asterisk are **FREE** via my website
—www.orlandoasanchez.com

ART SHREDDERS

I want to take a moment to extend a special thanks to the ART SHREDDERS.

No book is the work of one person. I am fortunate enough to have an amazing team of advance readers and shredders.

Thank you for giving of your time and keen eyes to provide notes, insights, answers to the questions, and corrections (dealing wonderfully with my extreme dreaded comma allergy). You help make every book and story go from good to great. Each and every one of you helped make this book fantastic, and I couldn't do this without each of you.

THANK YOU

ART SHREDDERS

Amber, Anne Morando, Audrey Cienki
  Beverly Collie
  Cat, Chris Christman II, Colleen Taylor
  Davina Noble, Dawn McQueen Mortimer, Denise King,

Diana Gray, Diane Craig, Dolly Sanchez, Donna Young Hatridge

Hal Bass, Helen

Jasmine Breeden, Jasmine Davis, Jeanette Auer, Jen Cooper, John Fauver, Joy Kiili, Joy Ollier, Julie Peckett

Karen Hollyhead

Larry Diaz Tushman, Laura Tallman I, Luann Zipp

Malcolm Robertson, Marcia Campbell, Maryelaine Eckerle-Foster, Melissa Miller

Paige Guido, Penny Campbell-Myhill

RC Battels

Sara Mason Branson, Sean Trout, Sondra Massey, Stacey Stein, Susie Johnson

Tami Cowles, Tanya Anderson, Ted Camer, Terri Adkisson, Tommy Owens

Wendy Schindler

ACKNOWLEDGEMENTS

With each book, I realize that every time I learn something about this craft, it highlights so many things I still have to learn. Each book, each creative expression, has a large group of people behind it.

This book is no different.

Even though you see one name on the cover, it is with the knowledge that I am standing on the shoulders of the literary giants that informed my youth, and am supported by my generous readers who give of their time to jump into the adventures of my overactive imagination.

I would like to take a moment to express my most sincere thanks:

To Dolly: My wife and greatest support. You make all this possible each and every day. You keep me grounded when I get lost in the forest of ideas. Thank you for asking the right questions when needed, and listening intently when I go off on tangents. Thank you for who you are and the space you create—I love you.

To my Tribe: You are the reason I have stories to tell. You cannot possibly fathom how much and how deeply I love you all.

To Lee: Because you were the first audience I ever had. I love you, sis.

To the Logsdon Family: The words *thank you* are insufficient to describe the gratitude in my heart for each of you. JL, your support always demands I bring my best, my A-game, and produce the best story I can. Both you and Lorelei (my Uber Jeditor) and now, Audrey, are the reason I am where I am today. My thank you for the notes, challenges, corrections, advice, and laughter. Your patience is truly infinite. *Arigato-gozaimasu.*

To The Montague & Strong Case Files Group—AKA The MoB (Mages of Badassery): When I wrote T&B there were fifty-five members in The MoB. As of this release, there are over one thousand five hundred members in the MoB. I am honored to be able to call you my MoB Family. Thank you for being part of this group and M&S.

You make this possible. **THANK YOU.**

To the ever-vigilant PACK: You help make the MoB...the MoB. Keeping it a safe place for us to share and just...be. Thank you for your selfless vigilance. You truly are the Sentries of Sanity.

Chris Christman II: A real-life technomancer who makes the **MoBTV LIVEvents +Kaffeeklatsch** on YouTube amazing. Thank you for your tireless work and wisdom. Everything is connected...you totally rock!

To the WTA—The Incorrigibles: JL, Ben Z. Eric QK., S.S., and Noah.

They sound like a bunch of badass misfits, because they are. My exposure to the deranged and deviant brain trust you all represent helped me be the author I am today. I have officially gone to the *dark side* thanks to all of you. I humbly give you my thanks, and...it's all your fault.

To my fellow Indie Authors, specifically the tribe at 20books to 50k: Thank you for creating a space where authors can feel listened to, and encouraged to continue on this path. A rising tide lifts all the ships indeed.

To The English Advisory: Aaron, Penny, Carrie, Davina, and all of the UK MoB. For all things English...thank you.

To DEATH WISH COFFEE: This book (and every book I write) has been fueled by generous amounts of the only coffee on the planet (and in space) strong enough to power my very twisted imagination. Is there any other coffee that can compare? I think not. DEATHWISH—thank you!

To Deranged Doctor Design: Kim, Darja, Tanja, Jovana, and Milo (Designer Extraordinaire).

If you've seen the covers of my books and been amazed, you can thank the very talented and gifted creative team at DDD. They take the rough ideas I give them, and produce incredible covers that continue to surprise and amaze me. Each time, I find myself striving to write a story worthy of the covers they produce. DDD, you embody professionalism and creativity. Thank you for the great service and spectacular covers. **YOU GUYS RULE!**

To you, the reader: I was always taught to save the best for last. I write these stories for **you**. Thank you for jumping down the rabbit holes of *what if?* with me. You are the reason I write the stories I do.

You keep reading...I'll keep writing.

Thank you for your support and encouragement.

CONTACT ME

I really do appreciate your feedback. You can let me know what you thought of the story by emailing me at:
orlando@orlandoasanchez.com

To get **FREE** stories please visit my page at:
www.orlandoasanchez.com

For more information on the M&S World...come join the MoB Family on Facebook!
You can find us at:
Montague & Strong Case Files

Visit our online M&S World Swag Store located at:
Emandes

If you enjoyed the book, **please leave a review**. Reviews help the book, and also help other readers find good stories to read.
THANK YOU!

Thanks for Reading
If you enjoyed this book, would you **please leave a review** at the site you purchased it from? It doesn't have to be a book report... just a line or two would be fantastic and it would really help us out!

Printed in Great Britain
by Amazon